The Clay Marble

and Related Readings

Glencoe McGraw-Hill

New York, New York   Columbus, Ohio   Woodland Hills, California   Peoria, Illinois

Acknowledgments

Grateful acknowledgment is given authors, publishers, photographers, museums, and agents for permission to reprint the following copyrighted material. Every effort has been made to determine copyright owners. In case of any omissions, the Publisher will be pleased to make suitable acknowledgments in future editions.

THE CLAY MARBLE by Minfong Ho. Copyright © 1991 by Minfong Ho. All rights reserved. Published by arrangement with Farrar, Straus & Giroux, Inc.

Adapted text excerpted from ENCHANTMENT OF THE WORLD: CAMBODIA by Miriam Greenblatt, Copyright © 1995 Children's Press, Inc., pp. 48–69. Reprinted by permission of Grolier Publishing Company.

from CHILDREN OF THE RIVER by Linda Crew. Copyright © 1989 by Linda Crew. Used by permission of Dell Publishing, a division of Random House, Inc.

from OLD WORLD MONKEYS by Ann Elwood, Copyright © 1989 Wildlife Education, Ltd. Reprinted by permission.

excerpt from TOYS MADE OF CLAY by Hannelore Schäl and Ulla Abdalla, translation by Mrs. Werner Lippmen and Mrs. Ruth Bookey. Copyright © 1990, 1987 Ravensburger Buchverlag Otto Maier GmbH, West Germany. Published in the U.S. by Children's Press®, Inc. Reprinted by permission of Grolier Publishing.

Text excerpt "The Shaping of *The Clay Marble*" by Minfong Ho, Copyright ® 1994. Reprinted by permission of the author.

Cover Art: Courtesy Monirith Chhea

Glencoe/McGraw-Hill

A Division of The **McGraw·Hill** Companies

Send all inquiries to:
Glencoe/McGraw-Hill
8787 Orion Place
Columbus, OH 43240

ISBN 0-02-818003-8
Printed in the United States of America
4 5 6 7 8 9 026 04 03

Contents

The Clay Marble

Contents *Continued*

iv

The Clay Marble

Minfong Ho

Preface

CAMBODIA'S LONG AND RICH HISTORY dates back over one thousand years, to when the magnificent Buddhist temple complex of Angkor was built. For centuries, Cambodia remained a powerful kingdom, periodically expanding and shrinking in border wars with neighboring Thailand, Laos, and Vietnam. In the last two centuries, it survived French colonialism and World Wars I and II relatively unscathed, and then managed to remain neutral throughout most of the Vietnam War.

During the 1970s, however, the United States, the Soviet Union, and China backed various political groups in Cambodia, and Cambodia became more and more polarized, until open conflict broke out.

In 1975, the same year the Communists "liberated" Vietnam, the Communist Khmer Rouge declared victory in Cambodia. What happened under that regime during the next four years was a nightmare for the Cambodian people. They were shut off from the rest of the world, and more than one million men, women, and children were killed. It wasn't until Vietnamese troops invaded Cambodia, and Cambodians had a chance to flee their country, that the outside world began to realize the awful suffering inflicted upon the Cambodians.

Night after night, scenes of gaunt, wide-eyed Cambodian refugees were broadcast on television news programs. Unable just to sit and watch, I took a leave of absence from Cornell University in the spring of 1980, and returned to Thailand, where I had grown up. There I joined an international relief agency and helped to set up supplementary feeding programs for children living in refugee camps along the Thai-Cambodian border.

I remember my first day at the Border. There are no words to describe the intensity of suffering I saw there. The sickness, the starvation, the sheer silence of this vast sea of people overwhelmed me. I wanted to shut my eyes, turn around, and go back home.

Then I felt a small hand on my arm. Looking up at me was a ragged little girl. She held one palm out to offer me a small round ball of mud. I took it, then impulsively bent down and scooped up some mud from a nearby puddle, and rolled my own clay marble. When she saw that I was offering her this marble in exchange for the one she had given me, her face broke out into a beautiful wide smile.

Within minutes, children were crowding around to show me their homemade toys—clay marbles and buffaloes, rag dolls, fish made from strips of banana leaves, trucks created out of tin cans. The intricacy of the toys was wonderful, but it was nothing compared to the radiance of those children's laughter.

I saw these refugees then for what they really were: not the victims of war but its victors. They were the people who had, against all odds, survived, determined to start their lives over again.

I don't know what happened to the little girl who gave me that clay marble. Maybe she went home to Cambodia with a fresh supply of rice and rice seed and tools, to try to make a new life for herself and her family. Or maybe she stayed on at the Border, one of a quarter-million other refugees still living in camps there.

Whatever she did, life could not have been easy for her. Today, Cambodia is still at war with itself, despite many attempts to come to a peaceful settlement.

The other evening, as I was strolling along the Mekong River just eighty miles upstream from Cambodia, I saw a group of children playing on the riverbank. They were rolling marbles out of the damp clay, and I stopped and asked for one. Smiling, they put a clay marble, still cool and damp, in my outstretched hand.

I have it on my desk. And although I have long since lost the other marble, I can hold this one, and look at the green rice plants swaying outside my open window here, and hope with all my heart that the little girl who gave me that first clay marble is safe and happy, home in Cambodia.

Minfong Ho
Vientiane, Laos, 1991

Chapter 1

I HEARD A COWBELL. At first it was such a faint tinkling sound that I thought it was just the wind in the trees, or the shrill cry of cicadas. I looked around. Dappled shadows stirred under a thick canopy of wild tamarind and rain trees, but there was no sign of life on the narrow trail stretching out ahead of us. I held my breath, and kept listening.

Yes. there it was again: the clear, quiet tone of a bronze bell.

"Sarun, listen!" I cried. "Can you hear it?"

My older brother turned to look at me. "Hear what?" he asked.

"A cowbell."

Sarun straightened up beside me in the oxcart and reined in the pair of oxen. Without the crunch of their hooves on the dry leaves, the forest seemed eerily quiet.

"I don't hear a thing," he said.

"I don't either, Dara," my mother added. She was sitting in the back of the cart behind us, on a thin layer of straw.

"Well, I heard it," I said. "A bronze cowbell. A big one—probably shiny, too." I could imagine it gleaming in the afternoon sunlight as it swung from the neck of a strong young bull.

"Which direction was it coming from?" Sarun asked. "Can you tell?"

I pointed to the reddish glow of afternoon sunlight filtering through the trees.

"Due west," my brother said thoughtfully, starting the oxen on their way again. "That's where we're headed. Maybe we're getting close to the Border."

"That's what you've been saying for days," I snapped, my hunger making me irritable.

Sarun glanced over at me and tried to smile. "Maybe we'll actually reach it tonight. Then we'll have grilled fish and fresh white rice for dinner. How does that sound?"

"I want something now," I said.

"But you just had breakfast," my mothr broke in gently. There was a bit of straw in her hair, and she looked tired and discouraged.

"That was just a handful of cold rice," I protested. "Besides . . ."

Sarun gave me a warning look. Quiet, it said, don't make Mother any unhappier.

I remained silent. The only sounds were the rustling of leaves above and the creaking of cartwheels beneath us.

Then my stomach growled. "We would have been better off if we had stayed at home," I mumbled.

Sarun heard me and looked annoyed. "Stayed home? For what?" he asked. "There's nothing there. No food, no seeds, no animals."

I thought of our village. Sarun was right, I admitted silently. It was just an expanse of dried-up rice fields now, with a crumbling temple and flimsy huts. In the latest spate of fighting, the Khmer Rouge soldiers had even set fire to our houses and rice barns, so that the invading Vietnamese soldiers wouldn't be able to claim them. But that had left us with nothing to eat, no rice seed with which to plant our next crop of rice, not even a house to live in.

It had not always been like that, though.

I remembered happier times, when I was just two or three years old, and the smiling round-faced Prince Sihanouk ruled Cambodia. Our little village was a peaceful and prosperous place then, the rice fields green and calm, the harvests plentiful. At weddings and on temple feast days, I had sat curled in my mother's warm lap, nibbling at some sticky rice and coconut, sleepily watching the familiar faces of my father and brother, cousins, aunts, and grandparents dancing by the light of a kerosene lamp in the temple courtyard.

But then the fighting and bombing had started. At first the war had been distant and mysterious. Tiny silver airplanes, like fishes in the sky, would fly over us before disappearing into the horizon. Then the bombing had come closer, so close that the bombs shook the soil beneath my bare feet. My father and the other farmers in our village dug trenches where we all hid, crouching at the sound of approaching planes. For months, bombs were dropped around us, sometimes as often as five or six times a day, and many of the villagers were killed or hurt by shrapnel.

Gaunt young Communist soldiers dressed in black came down from the hills to tell us that it was the American imperialists who were bombing us. Kill the imperialists, they exhorted us, and kick out Prince Sihanouk. But that was like being told to catch evil spirits—so faceless and far away were the pilots in their airplanes and the Prince in his palace.

Yet, remote as they seemed, they must have been defeated, because the bombing stopped. Soon the Communist soldiers took over the village, announcing that they had "liberated" us.

Liberation turned out to be a long nightmare of hunger and misery. And fear—always that cold, silent fear.

My brother and most of the other young men in our village were sent miles away to dig ditches with huge work crews. Most of the women and children were allowed to remain at home, but we had to work much harder than before, and always under the watchful eyes of the armed soldiers. We never got enough to eat, and were sometimes fed only rice gruel and boiled banana stalks at dawn and dusk.

One night my father was roused from his sleep and taken away by two soldiers. We found his body the next day, at the edge of the forest. Had he been killed because he knew how to read and write and had taught the village children their alphabet? Or perhaps because he had gone to catch some snails in the fields for my grandmother to eat because she was sick and dying? I will never know. I knew only that I was not allowed to ask about him, or even cry when I missed him.

Over and over again we had been told by the Khmer Rouge soldiers that Cambodia was one big family, and that the Communist Party was our parent. And yet, in trying to create a new "family," the Communists destroyed my own family, ripping apart parent from child, brother from sister, husband from wife. It made no sense to me, since I could not understand how these shrill young soldiers could be my parents, but I did not dare ask.

Three years passed like one long nightmare, the kind where you are gripped by such a cold dread that you are unable to wake up from it.

Finally, shortly after I turned twelve, Vietnamese soldiers in green uniforms marched into our village, sending Pol Pot's Khmer Rouge soldiers on the run, and "liberated" us again. In the confusion, while the two armies were busy fighting each other, Sarun and some other farm boys escaped from their work crew and made their way home.

What a strange reunion that was—so muted and sad.

Father was dead, Mother told Sarun. And Grandmother as well. Describing how other relatives had died or disappeared, Mother started to weep, but Sarun stopped her. "It's not time to grieve yet," he said. "This is our chance to save what's left of our family. The Khmer Rouge butchers are in retreat, and the new Vietnamese-controlled regime doesn't seem to have much power over us yet. We've got to try and put our own lives in order now."

And he told us of his plans to cross overland through western Cambodia to the border between our country and Thailand. He had heard rumors of a refugee camp called Nong Chan, located on the Thai-Cambodian border, where free food and tools were being handed out. "Thousands of farmers all over Cambodia have made their way there," he told us. "That's our only hope, to go there and stock up on food and rice seed and other supplies. Then we can come home, repair the house, replant our fields, start our lives over again."

Mother shook her head wearily. "How can we know if the fighting will ever stop?" she asked. "Or if the Khmer Rouge won't win back control of the country? How will we know that we can ever live in peace?"

"We won't know, Mother," Sarun said gently. "But at least we can try."

Quietly my mother looked at the scorched earth around her and then, without another word, dug up her small silver amulet of the Lord Buddha from where she had buried it years ago beside the bamboo grove. Then we hitched up our oxcart and started the long journey westward.

That was nine days ago, and our meager supply of food and our strength were running low. Yet there was still no sign of this Border. Instead, we had caught so many glimpses of fighting and bloodshed on the main roads that we decided to take to the small dirt paths winding through the forests. Sometimes we met other people traveling in small silent groups, on foot or in oxcarts like ours. But beyond exchanging a cautious greeting or some brief directions, no one ever talked to us. Once we met some Vietnamese soldiers on patrol who saw us before we could hide, but they made no attempt to stop us.

By Sarun's calculations, we should have been at this refugee camp at the Border two days ago. I stole a glance at him now. What if he was wrong, and there was no such thing? The thick forest stretched out in front of us quiet and dark. There seemed to be no end to it.

Then I heard it again, the distinct sound of a clear bronze bell in the distance. It was coming closer. I sat up straight and noticed that Sarun had cocked him head toward the sound. So he had heard something, too.

Then I saw it.

Smooth and polished, the bronze bell flashed in the afternoon sun. It was dangling from the neck of a milk-white Brahman bull, who slowly emerged from the shadows of some teak trees.

"I told you!" I said triumphantly.

Sarun just stared, awestruck.

The bull was pulling a cart heaped high with gunnysacks of rice, with plowshares, with hoe heads, with rope and even fishnets. So heavily laden was the cart that it swayed from side to side as it moved, creaking noisily.

As we watched, the wheels of the oxcart slipped into a deep rut and lodged there. The driver stood up in the cart and flicked his whip at the ox, urging it to pull. Nostrils flared, the bull strained at its harness. But it was no use. The cart did not budge.

Sarun jumped down from our oxcart and ran over to the other wagon. Nodding briefly at the driver, he gripped one of the spokes in the stuck wheel and began to push. The other man climbed down and joined him. For some time there was only the sound of grunts as both men applied their weight on either side of the large wooden wheel. Then slowly, inch by inch, they eased it out of the rut, and the cartwheel rolled free.

The stranger wiped the sweat off his forehead with his sleeve. "Thanks, brother," he said.

"It's nothing," Sarun replied. "That's quite a load you have there."

The man laughed. "Everything a person could want," he said.

Sarun circled the cart. There was a small tear in one of the sacks, and he squeezed somehing out of the slit, onto his hand. I heard him gasp.

"What is it?" I asked.

Wordlessly he came over to me and stretched out his hand. Cupped in his palm were some grains of rice, each one still encased in a protective shell of thin, brown husk.

"Rice seed," he said, his voice soft with wonder.

My heart leaped: rice seed. Rice not just to eat but to grow. Looking at the brown husks cupped in my brother's hand, I felt that we could really go home and plant a good crop after all.

"Where did you get this?" Sarun was asking the other man. "Is there any more?"

"Any more? Brother, is there any more water in the sea? Is there any more soil on the ground?" The man laughed again, a deep, throaty laugh. "There's more rice there than I've ever seen in my life!

Husked rice, long rice, short rice, sticky rice, fragrant rice . . .”

“And rice seed?” Sarun prompted.

“Rice seed? Listen, if they stacked up all the bags of rice seed there, they’d have a pile as high as the Cardamom Mountains!”

“And all this was at the Border?” Sarun asked.

“It’s not just rice, brother,” the other man went on. “Why, they’ve got enough tools there to build another Angkor Temple, and enough fishnets to catch all the fish in Tonle Sap Lake!”

“Tell me where!” Sarun asked, his voice urgent. “Was it at the Border?”

“Of course,” the stranger said. “At Nong Chan.”

Sarun swallowed hard. “Nong Chan?” he repeated. I could see the lump in his throat bob up, then down. “It’s true, then? Those rumors of free food and supplies at the refugee camp. It’s all true?” It was not really a question but a plea.

I realized then that despite my brother’s assurances to us, he must have had doubts all along.

The stranger sensed the tension in Sarun and grew serious. “If I laughed too much just now,” he said, “it was not because I was joking. No, it’s just that the happiness keeps jumping out of my throat. Yes, brother, it’s all true, what they say about the Border.”

“And there’s more there? For free?”

“Just stand in line, and they practically throw things at you,” the man said, and laughed again.

Behind me, I saw my mother bow her head over her silver amulet and pray. “Thanks be to the Lord Buddha,” she whispered.

And although for the past three years I had not prayed, so that now I could barely remember the words with which to speak to the Buddha, I bent my head and gave thanks, too.

Chapter 2

THE LAST RAYS OF AFTERNOON SUN were filtering through the forest as we approached the Border. Gradually the trees thinned out and the path widened. Several trails merged into ours. It seemed as if all the paths out of Cambodia were converging on this one spot on the Thai border.

I could barely contain my excitement. I imagined mountains of rice lining the horizon, and piles of tools and fishnets everywhere. Perhaps there would even be mounds of sweet moist coconut cakes and banana fritters. "Hurry," I urged my brother.

Yet, as we finally emerged from the forest, all we could see was a vast barren plain dotted with shrubs and scraggly trees, flat and desolate. Overgrown clumps of fireweed and red sorrel stuck out from patches of buffalo clover, and then even those gave way to the cracked, hard soil of paddy fields in the dry season.

As we drove farther through the scrubland, though, I noticed that there were signs of life in the distance, of people and oxcarts so far away that at first they looked like black specks. Sarun urged our oxen on, and soon we could see more evidence of human activity. The branches of the few trees around had been chopped bare for firewood, mudholes had been dug for buffaloes to wallow in, and makeshift fences had been built around small vegetable gardens. We drove past these and approached the fringe of the refugee camp itself. It looked like an endless brown sea of thatched lean-tos, mingled with bright blue patches from clusters of plastic tents. Spirals of smoke from countless cooking fires broke up the vast flatness of the landscape.

We passed women taking down laundry from lines, children spinning tops near the makeshift shelters, and quiet groups of people sitting around chatting. Why did it look so familiar and yet so unusual?

And it suddenly struck me: everyone was part of some family—not the cold-blooded Khmer Rouge version, the state as family, but a living, laughing, loving family.

I looked around in wonder. Even though many people seemed to be only fragments of a family—a frail grandmother with several young toddlers, or a group of young boys clustered around a few old men—they were a family just the same. Like a patchwork blanket, I thought, the people here were survivors of families who had been ripped apart and then joined again.

And everyone seemed to be busy doing something. Not just sitting alone silent and hollow-eyed with hunger, or organized into huge groups digging endless ditches. No, the people here were preoccupied with countless different chores of their own. I saw a sinewy old man splitting firewood; children lining up to draw buckets of water from a well; boys scrubbing their buffaloes in a shallow mudhole nearby; sisters combing each other's hair. And because it was getting close to dinnertime, there were women cooking everywhere. I could smell rice steaming, salted fish sizzling in hot oil spiced with chili, peanuts roasting—I even thought I caught a whiff of coconut cakes!

"It's like coming home," Mother said, with quiet wonder.

I knew exactly what she meant. Nong Chan was a strange place unlike anything we had ever seen before, a vast barren field teeming with refugees. But in the bustling quiet of dusk, it had the feel of our village during the years of peace before the fighting had started, when farmers would come in from the fields as their wives fanned the charcoal fires and their children bathed with fresh well water.

Driving our oxcart, Sarun maneuvered the oxen through the scattered campsites until it became too crowded for the animals to move easily. He jumped down and led the oxen by the reins, threading his way carefully among the families. He headed for a well near a forked tree, where there was also a shallow creek in which buffaloes were wallowing. Several clusters of people were already settled there, with their thatched lean-tos and small fires, but nearby there was some empty space that no family had staked out for its own yet.

"This looks like a good spot," Sarun said, turning to Mother. "It's only going to get more crowded farther in."

Mother nodded, and together we got off the cart and started to unload our few belongings while Sarun unhitched the oxen.

"Poor things, you've both earned a rest," he murmured to them, patting the animals' thin flanks as he led them off to the water hole nearby.

Mother looked around for a place to set down her kettle and sleeping mat.

A girl spoke up. "Put your things over here, if you like." She was kneeling, stirring a pot of bubbling rice, and smiling up at us.

Mother set down the kettle she was holding, and I helped her put her sleeping mat beside it.

"Welcome to Nong Chan," the girl said. She looked about Sarun's age, eighteen or nineteen, and had a broad face with high cheekbones. There was a bright checkered kerchief wrapped around her hair, and her eyes were friendly and curious. "Where do you come from?" she asked.

"Siem Reap," Mother answered.

"Really?" The girl brightened. "So do we! Our village is right next to the lake."

"That makes us practically neighbors," Mother said, squatting down companionably beside the girl. "How many of you have come over to the Border?"

"There's four of us: my grandfather and my two little cousins," the girl said.

"And your parents?"

"Dead," the girl said simply. "As are my sisters, and the parents of the cousins with us." She gave the pot of rice a quick stir. "My grandmother and three brothers, too. All dead."

"My husband died four years ago, and then my mother," Mother said.

For a moment there was silence. I had heard enough of such conversations not to interrupt. First there were the greetings, then the terse tally of the dead, then the pause. Only after that, it seemed, could there be talk of other things.

The girl fanned the cooking fire before dipping a twig into it. "Let me help you get your fire started," she said. "It's getting late, and you must be very hungry." She extended the glowing twig to my mother.

Mother looked at the twig, but made no move to accept it. "There's really no need," she said awkwardly. "We really . . . I mean, we don't . . ." We don't have any more rice to cook, I knew she wanted to say, except that she couldn't bring herself to admit it.

"Of course!" the girl exclaimed. "You don't have any firewood. How could you have gathered any? You just got here. Kindling is getting scarce, I can tell you. Most of the trees have been stripped bare—even the roots have been dug up for firewood. Here." She shoved a bundle of kindling toward Mother. "Use this for your fire."

Mother bit her lips. "No," she said, almost curtly. "You keep it."

The girl frowned, then her expression cleared. "Grandpa says my tongue's quicker than a raging river, but my mind is as thick as mud!" Using a tin cup, she scooped rice out of a gunnysack and stirred the grains into the pot already on the fire. "It's a good thing I just started cooking," she said cheerfully. "Won't have to start another pot. I'll just add some more water, and we'll have enough for all of us. There!" She looked up at me and my mother. "You will join us for dinner," she said. It wasn't a question, or even an invitation, but a simple statement.

"No, it's all right," my mother said stiffly. "We're not hungry."

The girl reached out and put her hand on Mother's arm. "You don't understand," she said gently. "It's different here. We have enough to eat. We have more than enough."

Then she must have seen the tears brimming over in Mother's eyes, because she turned away and started to stir the rice vigorously.

Before long the girl had Mother peeling a clove of garlic and crushing dried red peppers. I could tell that my mother was enjoying cooking again, now that there was seasoning and even some salted dried fish to work with.

Next the girl turned her attention to me. "I'm going to bathe while the rice is cooking," she said. "Want to come along, little sister?"

I heistated.

"Not shy, are you? My name's Nea. What's yours?"

"Dara."

"Well, come on, Dara. I've got a bucket of clean well water here we could share."

There was nothing I would have liked more than to douse myself with cool water just then, but I could see no hedge, no mud-brick wall, not even a line of laundry, to bathe behind.

Nea must have sensed my shyness, because she laughed as she tugged at me. "You've got to do everything out in the open here," she said cheerfully. "Come on, it's easy once you get used to it."

I followed Nea as she carried her pail of water to a massive beam of solid stone half-sunken in the fields. "My grandfather says that it might have been the crossbeam over the gateway of an ancient temple during the Angkor Empire," Nea said, pointing to the stone. "If so, it'd be almost a thousand years old."

I looked at the stone beam curiously. Chiseled on it were some whorled markings, worn smooth with time. On one corner of it was a carving of what must have been an apsara, a dancing angel. But all that remained now was a delicate hand, its stone fingers arching gracefully back as if in the middle of a dance. Gently I touched one fingertip, and felt as if I had reached across a thousand years.

"How did it get here?" I asked.

"Grandpa Kem isn't sure. Maybe it was the spoils of war, taken from some famous faraway temple like Angkor, or maybe there are some small ruins nearby that nobody even knows about."

Then, without even looking around, Nea hitched her sarong up to her breasts and deftly stripped off her shirt. Scooping some water out of her bucket with a dipper, she splashed the water over her bare shoulders.

"Come on," she called, sprinkling some on me.

How wonderfully cool the drops of water felt. Clumsily I wrapped my sarong around my chest, too. Just as well I'm still flat-chested, I thought, as I wriggled out of my shirt.

Together, taking turns with the dipper, we bathed out in the open. I scooped ladle after ladle of water over myself, feeling the cold seeping through my scalp and down my shoulders. After those long, dusty days in the creaky oxcart, it felt so refreshing that I laughed out loud, and Nea laughed along with me.

When we had used up all the water, we walked back toward the carts, swinging the empty pail between us. As we approached the cooking fire, Mother looked up at us and smiled. I felt as if someone had suddenly reached inside me and squeezed my heart, so strong and happy was my mother's smile. I couldn't remember when I'd last seen her smile like that.

"Dinner's ready," Mother announced, pointing to a dish of salted fish stir-fried in garlic, and the pot of steaming rice. "Hope I didn't make it too spicy."

I started to head for the food, but felt Nea tugging at the pail.

"Come on," she was saying nervously. "Let's get into some dry clothes."

Only then did I notice that my brother was nearby, and staring open-mouthed at us. Not at me, I realized, just at Nea. I looked at my new friend. Beads of water glistened on her bare shoulders, and her wet sarong clung to her. I felt annoyed at my brother for staring like that, but one look at him, and I relented. All those years Sarun had spent digging ditches, I thought, he'd probably never seen a girl as lovely as Nea. Or as wet.

By the time I had changed into dry clothes, and joined my mother and brother by the cooking fire, an old man and two children were also sitting there. Mother edged closer to Sarun to make room for me, so that the three of us formed a semicircle around the flames.

Nea started ladling out the rice, and as she did so, she introduced the old man next to her, a tall gruff man with thick eyebrows. "This is Bou Kem, my grandfather," she said.

I nodded at him shyly.

"What do you say?" Mother prompted me.

"Grandpa Kem," I said obediently, and Mother nodded her approval.

On her other side, Nea explained, were her two cousins. One was a girl about my own age, and the other was a plump baby. I barely nodded to each of them before turning my attention to the rice.

Nea handed the first plateful to her grandfather, who took it without comment. She passed the next plate to my mother, who hesitated, then thanked her softly. Sarun was next. When Nea stretched out her hands to offer him a plate, he would not take it.

"Sarun, come on," I whispered.

He pretended not to hear me, and kept stoking the fire, sending a few sparks spinning up into the air. Torn between his hunger and his pride, Sarun couldn't seem to decide whether to accept or refuse Nea's offering.

"Please eat something, brother," Nea said softly, smiling at him across the fire. "It has been a long hard trip, and you need to keep your strength up."

He looked up at her, and finally he held out his hands and accepted the plate of rice from her.

My turn was next, and I almost snatched the plate from Nea. The fragrance of the long-grained rice was wonderful. Steamy and sweet and warm, it wafted up to me. I had not seen such a generous mound of white rice for a long, long time.

I lifted a spoonful of rice and ate it. I thought about what a wonderful thing it is to eat rice. First you let the smell drift up in lazy spirals, sweet and elusive; then you look at the color of it, softer and whiter than the surrounding steam. Carefully you put a spoonful of it in your mouth, and feel each grain separate on your tongue, firm and warm. Then you taste it—the rich yet delicate sweetness of it. How different it was from that gritty red rice we'd been rationed to, the last three years, gruel so bland and watery that it slipped right down your throat before you could even taste it. No, this was real rice, whole moist grains I could chew and savor.

I thought I was slowly relishing each mouthful, but before I knew it, my plate was empty. My mother had already started her second plateful, and Sarun was finishing off his third. None of my family had even bothered to try the fish in garlic sauce, we were enjoying the plain rice so much. I wondered if we were being too greedy. But Nea had noticed my empty plate and was already reaching over to ladle more rice on it.

"What about you?" Mother asked, glancing at the rest of Nea's family. "Will there be enough?"

"There's more than enough." Nea smiled. "That's what makes the rice taste so sweet here, don't you think?"

Nobody else said anything much, and soon we were all done eating. Mother went off with Nea's young cousin to rinse off the plates at the well, while Sarun stayed by the fire to talk to Nea and her grandfather.

I strolled back to our oxcart and shook out my sleeping mat. Ever since we'd set out on this trip, I had slept under the broad wooden planks of the cart. In the unfamiliar darkness of the forest, it had been comforting to have those planks as a shelter. But I hesitated now, standing with my mat between the cartwheels.

Close by, the cooking fire was burning low, and a few sparks still whirled away into the night sky. Elsewhere, a boy was whittling a stick of firewood, and a baby was whimpering as its mother crooned to it.

On an impulse, I decided that I wanted to sleep under the open sky. So I spread my mat alongside the cart and stretched out on it.

The stars were just beginning to shine, and a cool evening breeze stirred the still air. In the distance, I heard a mother singing a lullaby. It had a familiar melody, one that I could remember my mother singing to me long ago. The pulsing hum of night sounds, of crickets and cicadas, settled over me like a light blanket.

As I shut my eyes, I took a deep breath. I had the strange feeling that somehow I had finally come back home.

Chapter 3

SOUNDS OF SPLASHING WATER and soft laughter drifted into my sleep. Drowsily I wondered who was taking a morning shower by the well in our bamboo grove at home. Then I blinked my eyes open, saw the silhouette of our oxcart wheel next to me, and remembered where I was.

The dawn sky was just beginning to glow, but already people were up and bustling about.

Nea was nearby, tending a cooking fire. Her face was as powdery-smooth as a lotus in bloom, and the morning light made her cheeks glow. Mother, too, looked refreshed and relaxed as she helped Nea fan the small fire.

I folded up my sleeping mat and stashed it in our oxcart. Quietly I walked over to them and sat down in my mother's lap. With her warmth behind me, and the flames in front of me, I felt very snug and secure.

"Really, Dara, you're too big to sit like this," Mother said, but she made no move to push me away. Instead, she started to stroke my hair.

Nea smiled at us. "Sleep well?" she asked.

I nodded, too content to say anything.

Mother held me for a while longer, then nudged me aside. "There must be something Dara could help with?" she asked Nea.

"Well, you could help carry some water back from the well," Nea suggested, smiling at me. "Jantu's there right now."

"Jantu?" I asked.

"My cousin. You met her last night, at dinner."

Vaguely I remembered the girl sitting across the fire from me, but at the time I had been too engrossed in the steaming white rice to pay her any attention. I had no idea what Jantu looked like.

"Don't worry, she'll recognize you," Nea said, laughing, as if guessing my thoughts. She handed me a bucket and waved me off toward the well.

I strolled past clusters of people, all busy preparing for a new day. There was nothing to mark one campsite from another, but I could sense where one family's space ended and another's began. Like rain-drops merging at the center of a lily pad, the members of each family gathered around their own cooking fire, a child often cradled in the lap of its mother's sarong. As far as I could see, the campsites stretched in every direction, their brown thatching relieved by flowered sarongs fluttering on laundry lines, or trays of red chili drying in the sun.

I soon reached the well. It had been dug in a small clearing and fenced in by a wall of scraggly branches. Pivoting on a tall post next to the well was a bamboo pole with a bucket dangling on the end. Dozens of children were lined up, waiting their turn to dip the bucket into the well. They all seemed to know one another, and there was a lot of jostling and teasing. I looked around for Jantu, but couldn't find her.

"Hey, over here!" I heard someone call. I turned and saw a tall, thin girl waving at me, with a chubby baby balanced on one hip. "You're Sarun's sister, right?" the girl asked.

I nodded.

"I'm Jantu," she said. Her shoulder-length hair was pulled back from her face and fastened with a shiny metal clasp. She brushed a strand of hair behind her ear impatiently as she looked at me. "How old are you?" she asked.

"Twelve," I said.

"Well, I'm thirteen," she announced smugly. Squinting against the light, she studied me for a moment. "Funny, you don't look much like your brother," she said. "He's good-looking, not like you." Behind her, some girls giggled.

I flushed. I had never thought of myself as pretty, but nobody had come this close to telling me I was actually ugly, either. I knew my sarong was muddy, and my hair uncombed, but another few buckets of well water would change all that.

I glared at Jantu and she watched me, grinning. I reached out and touched the baby's foot. "This your brother?" I asked her.

Jantu nodded, with a touch of pride.

"He's cute," I said. "Not like you."

The same girls who had just now giggled at me burst out laughing. For a moment Jantu looked taken aback, then she joined in the laughter, her eyes crinkling up.

I relaxed.

The baby started to squirm, and Jantu shifted him over to her other hip and jiggled him to keep him quiet. He had big round eyes and a thick thatch of shiny black hair. I reached out and tickled him. He squealed in delight.

"What's his name?" I asked.

"Nebut, but we just call him Baby. I take him to the lunch truck every day," Jantu said proudly. "That's why he's so chubby."

"What's the lunch truck?" I asked.

Jantu studied me a moment. "You could do with some visits to it yourself," she said. "That's where you get a free meal—a hot one. Any child who stands in line at one of the feeding stations gets a plate of food from the relief officials. You just bring your own plate and spoon. And the food's great! Yesterday we had eggplant curry over rice." She rubbed her brother's round tummy and smiled. "Didn't we, Baby?"

I wasn't sure what Jantu was talking about, but before I could ask, it was our turn at the well. Jantu grabbed her bucket and walked to the pole by the well. As I hesitated, she turned around and flashed me a grin. "Come on, I'll show you what to do," she said. "Just follow me!"

After we had filled our buckets, I followed her back to our camp-site. The four grownups were sitting around the fire, eating some of the leftover rice from dinner, and Jantu and I joined them.

After breakfast, Sarun started building a shelter nearby, hammering four bamboo poles into the ground and tying cross-poles over them. Mother draped some thatched roofing over the cross-poles, while Nea stitched together more roofing from palmetto leaves.

"Dara! Come help us," Mother called.

Soon I had strung up a laundry line between our cart and Nea's, and my spare sarong was flapping gaily in the breeze.

As a finishing touch, my brother hung a cloth hammock from the branches of a teak sapling nearby and invited Jantu and me to sit on it. As we sat there, swinging gently back and forth, I felt that I had settled down quite happily at the Border.

We were still swinging on the hammock early that afternoon when Jantu sat up and claimed that she could hear the faint rumble of the food truck.

"Come on!" she shouted, jumping off the hammock so abruptly that I nearly fell off. She rushed to her tent and grabbed a tin plate and spoon with one hand and her baby brother with the other.

"Hurry up!" she called. "And bring your own plate with you!"

With that she was off, running toward the sound of the truck, her brother bouncing up and down on her hip. I picked up my tin plate and spoon and followed her.

As we ran, we were joined by dozens of other children. They darted out of tents, from beneath oxcarts, and down trees, waving spoons and plates in the air as they headed toward the main road. From a tent nearby one little boy emerged clutching a bowl. His trousers slipped down from his waist as he started to run, almost tripping him. For a few steps he tried to hold on to his trousers as well as the bowl, then gave up and left his trousers on the ground in a heap, before continuing stark naked. I laughed, and kept running after Jantu.

I could see the food truck now. Churning up clouds of dust, it careened down the winding dirt road, stopping next to a signpost that had a big red "3" written on it.

"Quick, we have to get in line!" Jantu shouted.

By the time we got to the truck there was already a big crowd of children there. I held on to Jantu's shirt as we jostled for a place.

Under the noonday sun, the string of children wound far across the bare, dusty fields. There must be hundreds of us here, I thought. Most were about five or six years old, but there were some older children as well. Like Jantu, they often carried a baby on their hip.

At the front of the line, two huge pots had been unloaded off the truck, and a burly man was ladling out food from them. Two other men stood nearby, hoisting the empty pots back to the truck and carrying more full ones down the ramp. A young woman in khaki trousers and short hair looked on from the truck, earnestly writing in her red notebook.

When my turn finally came, I held out my plate just as all the other children in front of me had done. My mouth watering, I watched the man ladle out a mound of steaming white rice and splash another ladleful of some yellow squash stew over it. Just the smell of that stew, I thought happily, could fill me up and float me away!

Behind me, Jantu awaited her turn. Patiently she held out her plate for her share of food, as I stood off to one side.

Then, careful not to spill even a drop of the stew, we threaded our way over to a bit of shade under an acacia tree and sat down. Jantu was very good to her brother, spoon-feeding him the best parts of the stew, even though I knew she must be hungry, too. As for me, I dug right in, wolfing down huge mouthfuls.

All around me were children eating, their heads bent over their plates. "You know," I said between mouthfuls, "my brother kept saying there'd be food at the Border, but I didn't quite believe him."

"And now you do."

"That's the strange thing. It's still hard for me to believe it," I said. "It's almost too good to be true."

Jantu laughed. "This is nothing," she said. "Wait till you see what they give out at the real food distributions—for the grownups. That's even better!"

I sat back, leaning against the tree, and breathed a deep sigh of contentment. There was a morsel of meat left on my plate, which I had been saving till last. Slowly I spooned it up and swallowed it. How could anything be better than this?

Chapter 4

THE VERY NEXT EVENING, when my family and Jantu's were gathered around the cooking fire for our dinner, the topic of the food distribution came up. As the grownups talked about it, I held Jantu's baby brother in my lap and listened quietly.

Every two weeks or so, Nea said, a convoy of massive trucks arrived at Nong Chan, bringing basic food supplies such as rice, cooking oil, and salted fish. "Until you get your rations, my family can share ours with you," she said. "That's what happens all over the camp: the families who arrived earlier sharing with those who come after them. It all works out in the end."

"But how do we get our own rations?" Sarun asked.

"Well, a few days before the trucks are due, word generally spreads around the whole camp that there will be a distribution soon. Then, as head of your family, you'll have to join up with a team of other refugee families. Each team then gets registered with the relief officials," Nea said. "I think there's due to be another distribution in about five or six days. You should join up with a team now so you can register for that distribution."

It all sounded rather complicated to me. "Could . . . could we join your team?" I asked shyly.

Nea laughed. It was a soft, melodious sound, like the faint tinkling of temple bells in the breeze. "Why not?" she said. "It feels as if we're already part of the same family, doesn't it?"

I nodded happily. Yes, that was exactly how it felt. Just living next to each other these last couple of days, sharing meals and chores and stories, our families, I felt, had grown very close.

Impulsively I held the baby up and hugged him. He felt heavy and solid. He squirmed and wriggled loose. Only then did I notice the warm, dark stain on my sarong where he had wet it. Laughing, I handed him back to Jantu.

Just as Nea had said, we soon heard that a convoy of trucks was due to arrive at Nong Chan by the end of the week. Sarun joined

Grandpa Kem's team and, along with the other men in their team, walked the two miles from the fringe of the refugee camp, where we were living, to the other edge, where the long thatched shelters of the camp headquarters had been built. There they registered their team with the relief officials, and were told to return in two days.

At dawn on the appointed day, when Sarun and Grandpa Kem hitched up one of the oxcarts, I begged to be allowed to go along, too. Much to my surprise, they agreed to take me.

Our team drove through the sprawling outskirts of Nong Chan on six oxcarts. I sat wedged between Sarun and Grandpa Kem on our cart. Craning my neck to see around, I began to understand how large the refugee camp was. I had heard the grownups estimate that there were at least forty thousand people here, but I had no sense of what that meant. Now I could see how the massive waves of refugees like ourselves had turned the flat, abandoned fields of Nong Chan into a teeming camp of thatched tents and plastic shelters that stretched out toward the horizon. If I were a tadpole weaving my way through a big, flooded seedbed, I thought, and each rice seedling were a refugee family, that might be about how big this camp is!

Finally we came to the heart of Nong Chan. Under tall bamboo watchtowers, we parked our oxcarts in a sandy lot packed with thousands of other people and their carts. All that morning we waited. It was hot and dry, and there wasn't a spot of shade anywhere, but nobody complained.

At about noon I saw a huge cloud of dust on the horizon. Soon a line of trucks roared down the dirt road that linked Nong Chan to the Thai town of Aranyaprathet, thirty miles away. The trucks ground to a halt in front of the entrance of the refugee camp, where the dirt road ended.

"Fifty-three trucks," Sarun said, his voice awed. "Now what?"

The tailgate of each truck swung down, and immediately groups of men with yellow armbands started unloading the sacks of rice, swinging and tossing the heavy gunnysacks from man to man with a swift, rhythmic motion.

As the rice was being unloaded and stacked into huge piles twice my height, officials with red armbands ushered the first registered team of men into corrals where sacks of rice had already been placed. Team by team, the men rushed in, hauled away the sacks allotted to them, and quickly left to make room for the next team.

I watched, awed by the almost clockwork precision of it all. There were thousands of men waiting before our turn came, but the distribution went so quickly and smoothly that we didn't have to wait long at all.

When it was our turn, and the bamboo gate of the corral was flung open to us, I climbed up and sat on the fence as the men on our team charged right through. I watched Grandpa Kem and Sarun carry a sack between them, staggering slightly under its weight. As soon as they reached the oxcart, they swung the sack up and over into the cart, then immediately went back for more. With the other men working as quickly and precisely, soon all our team's oxcarts were fully loaded.

Gasping for breath, Sarun wiped the sweat from his forehead with his checkered scarf as he eyed the filled oxcarts. "Now let's go show the women what we've got!" he said. As if he were heading a triumphal procession, he drove the team's first oxcart back through Nong Chan as the others rumbled behind.

As we approached our campsite, I saw Jantu jump up from the hammock and heard her shout, "They're back!"

In a flash, Nea and Mother and a dozen other women dashed out of their shelters, craning their necks toward us. Saran sat up tall and straight next to Grandpa Kem and me. He was trying to look dignified, but when he saw Mother running up to greet him, he broke into a wide smile. "Look in the cart," he told her gleefully, reining the oxen to a stop.

Inside our cart were large, bulging gunnysacks, stacked neatly on top of one another.

"Rice!" Mother said softly.

"Yes, and something else, too," he said. His eyes searched the crowd until he found Nea. She was standing a little apart from the crowd, her face framed by a bright scarf. Looking straight at her, he pointed at the gunnysack next to him. "Something special," he said to Nea. "Look."

"Fragrant rice?" Nea asked, making her way toward our cart for a look.

"Even better than that," he said, waiting for her to come closer.

It was only when she got within a few steps of us that she made out the words stenciled in green on the sack. "Rice seed," she read out loud, and looked up at Sarun with shining eyes.

"A special rice seed," Sarun said. "We were told by the officials that it has been treated against insects and mildew, so that almost each grain should germinate. And it's of a fragrant, high-yielding variety of rice, too."

Nea looked impressed. Stepping up to the cart, she touched the sack of rice seed and said, "You have so much of it. Three sacks?"

"Four," Sarun said proudly. "And we were also told that at the next distribution there would be hoe heads, and fishnets as well!" He jumped down from the cart and stood smiling beside her. "We can really plan ahead now, for the next planting season."

Nea looked up at him, then demurely lowered her eyes. Her voice was soft when she spoke. "You'll need help, planting all that rice seed," she said.

"I hope to find some help, sowing and transplanting it," Sarun answered. I had never heard his voice so gentle before. I jumped off the cart and edged toward them, not wanting to miss a word.

"Your mother and sister can help," Nea was saying.

"My mother is getting old, and my sister is still young," Sarun answered.

"You'll have friends from your village who'll be glad to help," Nea said. "Strong friends. Pretty ones, too."

"I think I have a friend right here," Sarun said, "who's stronger and much prettier than anyone back home."

Listening to them, I was reminded of the village folk dances at harvesttime, when the pairs of young men and women would dance the ramwong, slowly circling each other, their fingertips sometimes touching.

"It's a good village," Sarun was saying, his voice soft and warm. "At the edge of Tonle Sap lake, where the soil is black and moist. Our harvests are good, and there's plenty of fish fresh from the lake." He paused and smiled at Nea. "You'd like it there," he said.

Nea started to walk away. "How can you be so sure that I'd like it there?" she asked, looking over her shoulder at my brother.

"There's only one way to find out," Sarun said, walking after her. "Come with me, when we go home."

I started to follow them but suddenly felt a sharp tug at my arm. Jantu stood beside me, trying to pull me away. I resisted, but she was stronger, and managed to drag me with her.

"But I wanted to listen to them!" I said angrily when we were some distance from Sarun and Nea.

"I know!" Jantu snapped, still gripping my arm. "But anybody could tell they wanted to be alone. Your mother moved off, didn't she? So did Grandpa Kem."

I hadn't noticed, but now that Jantu mentioned it, I saw that my mother had quietly retreated to her own thatched lean-to, and Grandpa Kem was talking to the other men. I frowned. "But why?" I asked.

Jantu gave me an impatient look. "Why else do you think a man and a woman might want to talk alone?" she asked.

Saran and Nea were strolling away from the oxcart, still deep in conversation. Nea's face glowed with a kind of bashful admiration, while Sarun gestured eagerly as he talked. They looked as if they were in a world of their own.

A startling new thought occurred to me. "You mean they're going to get married?" I blurted out.

Jantu grinned. "Who knows? The monsoons won't start for weeks yet and we have to go home to plant the rice crop," she said. "A lot could happen before then!"

I looked at the oxcart Sarun had driven back. The other team members were now dividing the sacks of rice and systematically carrying them off into the shelters of the various families. Soon we would be heading home with farm tools, new fishnets, and rice seed to start a new crop, a new life. I felt a quiver of anticipation and joy so strange to me that it was a while before I recognized it for what it was: a sense of hope.

Chapter 5

THE DAYS AT THE BORDER passed quickly. I enjoyed spending my time with Jantu, since she was usually outgoing and friendly. Sometimes she would come up with new ideas about what to play, and sometimes she would just sit in the shade and tell me stories.

What I enjoyed listening to most were the folktales she told, some of which I had heard before from my own grandmother, but many of which were new to me. One of my favorites was about Khong the Brave, a coward who bragged that he had killed a tiger when it was actually his wife who had beaten it to death. "How can a woman kill a tiger?" he sneered. "I'm the one who did it!" When the King heard about it, Khong was commanded to lead the Cambodian army into battle on a huge elephant. In his terror, Khong accidentally jabbed the elephant's eye with his spear. Howling in rage and pain, the elephant charged into the enemy ranks, scattering them, and Khong the Brave became a true hero.

Jantu would pace back and forth excitedly as she told the story, her eyes sparkling as she acted out the part of the tiger, then Khong, then the elephant, all the while bouncing her baby brother on her hip. I would listen to her, spellbound, amid a small audience of other children.

Sometimes Jantu also used folktales to explain things to me. Not all children grow up with one war being fought after another, she said. In other places, and even in Cambodia during peacetime, children grew up without seeing a single soldier! Then why are there all these different armies fighting each other now, I asked. Even on the Border, there were separate military base camps made up of Khmer Rouge soldiers, Khmer Serei soldiers, and Khmer People's National Liberation soldiers, not to mention the Vietnamese soldiers to the east and the Thai soldiers to the west—all fighting one another. None of it made any sense to me.

"Don't you know the story about the family of deaf men?" Jantu answered, a mischievous gleam in her eye. Four deaf brothers, she said, were living together quite happily until a crocodile wandered into their house.

The oldest deaf brother shouted out a warning, pointing to the crocodile.

The second deaf brother, seeing his elder brother with the crocodile, thought they were going to attack him, and grabbed a stick to defend himself.

The third deaf brother thought the other two were planning to kill him, snatched up a knife, and brandished it around.

When the fourth deaf brother saw his brothers waving their weapons at the crocodile, he threw a rock at it. The rock bounced off the crocodile's hide and hit one of the brothers. Within seconds, all four deaf brothers were screaming and fighting each other as the crocodile slipped out the door.

"You see?" Jantu concluded with a shrug. "The leaders of Cambodia are just like those four deaf brothers, fighting among themselves because they cannot hear one another."

As much as I loved listening to the stories she told, what fascinated me even more were the things she made.

It amazed me, the way she shaped things out of nothing. A knobby branch, in her deft hands, would be whittled into a whirling top. She would weave strips of a banana leaf into plump goldfish or angular frogs. A torn plastic bag and a scrap from some newspaper would be cut and fashioned into a graceful kite with a long tail. A couple of old tin cans and a stick would be transformed into a toy truck.

Whenever Jantu started making something, she would withdraw into her own private world and ignore everything around her. Leaving me to mind her baby brother, she would hunch over her project, her fierce scowl keeping at bay anybody who might come too close or become too noisy. But if I was quiet and kept my distance, she didn't seem to mind my watching her.

And so I would stand a little to one side, holding the baby on my hip, as Jantu's quick fingers shaped, twisted, smoothed, rolled whatever material she happened to be working with into new toys.

"How do you do it?" I asked her one day, after she had casually woven me a delicate bracelet of wild vines.

"Well, you take five vines of about the same length—elephant creeper vines like this work well—and you start braiding them, see. Like this . . ."

"No, I don't mean just this bracelet," I said. "I mean the goldfish, too, and the kites and toy trucks and . . ."

"But they're all different," Jantu said. "You make them different ways."

"But how do you know what to make? Is there some . . . some kind of magic in your hands, maybe?"

Jantu looked puzzled. "I don't know," she said, turning her hands over and examining them with vague interest. They looked like ordinary hands, the fingernails grimy, the palms slightly callused. "I don't see anything there," she said. "Nothing that looks like magic." She shrugged and dismissed the subject.

Yet the more I watched her, the more convinced I became that Jantu's hands were gifted with some special powers, some magic. How else could anyone explain how she made that wonderful mobile, of two delicate dolls husking rice?

Even from the start, I knew it was going to be something special. For three days Jantu had kept me busy scrounging up a collection of old cloth and string. Then, as I sat cross-legged watching her, she fashioned two straw dolls in sarongs and straw hats and, with dabs of sticky rice, glued their feet onto a smooth branch. Carefully she tied strings connecting the dolls' wrists and waists, so that when one doll bent down, the other one straightened up. Each doll held a long thin club, with which, in turn, one would pound at a tiny mortar as the other doll lifted up its club in readiness. Jantu held up the mobile and showed me how a mere breath of wind would set the two dolls in motion.

Pound and lift, up and down, the two dolls took turns crushing the rice with exactly the same jerky rhythm that real village women pounded it to get the brown husks off. There were even some real grains in the miniature mortar set between the two dolls. It was the cleverest thing I had ever seen.

Children crowded around Jantu, pressing in from all sides to watch her work it. "Let me hold it," I begged, standing next to Jantu. "I helped you find the stuff for the dolls."

Jantu nodded. Breathlessly I held it carefully and blew on it. It worked! One of the dolls bent down and pounded the mortar with its club. The other doll straightened up and waited its turn. I was still engrossed with it when someone shouted a warning: "Watch out, Chnay's coming!"

Even in my short stay at the camp, I'd heard of Chnay. He liked to break things, and he was a bully. An orphan, Chnay had made his way to the Border alone. Too young to be recruited into the resistance army, Chnay roamed the fields by himself, scrounging for food and sleeping wherever he liked.

Chnay sauntered up and shoved his way through to us. "What've you got there?" he demanded.

"Nothing," I said, trying to hide the toy behind me.

Laughing, Chnay snatched it away from me. One of the dolls was ripped loose and dropped to the ground.

As I bent over to retrieve it, Chnay pushed me aside. "Leave it," he said. "That's for kids. Look what I have." He thrust his arm out. It was crawling with big red ants, the fierce kind that really sting when they bite. "I'm letting them bite me. See?" he bragged. Already small fierce welts were swelling up on his arm, as some ants kept biting him.

"That's dumb!" I exclaimed. Dodging behind him, I tried to snatch the mobile back from him.

Chnay flung the toy to the ground, scattering straw and red ants into the air.

I grabbed on to his hand, but he was taller than I, and much stronger. He shoved me aside and stomped on the dolls until they were nothing but a pile of crushed sticks and rags. Then, kicking aside a boy who stood in his way, Chnay strode off, angrily brushing red ants off his arm.

I squatted down beside the bits of dolls and tried to fit them together, but it was no use. The delicate mobile was beyond repair. I could feel my eyes smarting with angry tears. "I should've held on to it more tightly," I said bitterly. "I shouldn't have let him grab it away from me."

Jantu knelt next to me and took the fragments of the dolls out of my hands. "Never mind," she said quietly, putting them aside. "We can always start something new."

"But it took you so long to make it," I said.

Idly Jantu scooped up a lump of mud from a puddle by her feet and began to knead it in her hands. "Sure, but the fun is in the making," she said.

She looked down at the lump of mud in her hands with sudden interest. "Have you ever noticed how nice the soil around here is?" she asked. "Almost like clay." She smoothed the ball with quick fingers, then rolled it between her palms.

When she opened her palm and held it out to me, there was a small brown ball of mud cupped in it. "For you," she announced.

I looked at it. Compared to the delicate rice-pounding mobile, this was not very interesting at all. "I don't want it," I said. "It's just a mud ball."

"No, it's not. It's a marble," Jantu said. Her eyes sparking, she blew on it. "There! Now it's a magic marble."

I took it and held it. Round and cool, it had a nice solid feel to it. I glanced at Jantu. She was smiling. Slowly I smiled back at her.

Maybe, I thought, maybe she did put some magic in the marble. After all, why else would I feel better, just holding it?

Chapter 6

AFTER THAT MARBLE, Jantu was interested only in playing with clay. She would spend the long afternoons crouched by the mud puddle by the stone beam, scooping up handfuls of moist clay to shape little figures.

For some reason, the massive stone beam attracted Jantu. She loved playing there. "It's so old, so solid," she said. "I like being near it. It makes me feel like a cicada molting under some big rain tree."

At one end of the stone beam she had propped some fantail palm fronds, to make a thatched shelter so that we could play in the shade. When we crouched under it, it was like being in a leafy cave.

We spent most of our spare time in there. I would sit on the stone beam, bouncing her baby brother in my lap, as Jantu sculpted her dainty clay figures.

"I wish we could always be together like this," I said one afternoon. "Don't you wish things would just stay the same?"

Jantu glanced up from the clay buffalo she was shaping and smiled at me. "But how can we always stay the same, Dara?" she asked. "We're not made of stone. You wouldn't want to lie half-buried in the fields for hundreds of years, anyway, would you?"

"No, I meant . . . I just meant that nothing nice ever lasts." I struggled to find words for what I wanted to say. "What we're doing now, just playing here together—I wish we could hang on to it, that's all."

Jantu put down the half-formed clay buffalo. "I know what you mean," she said slowly. "You try to hang on to older people—parents, uncles, grandmothers—and they disappear. You make friends, and they go off in different directions, never to be seen again. Everything crumbles, so easily." Absentmindedly she picked up a dirt clod and crushed it in her fist, letting the crumbs of dirt dribble out. "We don't even have real families anymore," she said. "Just bits and pieces of one."

I stole a glance at my friend. I knew Jantu had lost both her parents and an older brother during the long war years, but she never talked about it.

"What do you mean?" I asked carefully.

"What I have, and what you have," she said, "are leftovers of families. Like fragments from a broken bowl that nobody wants. We're not a real family."

"What's a real family, then?"

"A real family," Jantu said, "grows. It gets bigger. People get added to it. Husbands, mothers-in-law, babies."

I thought about this. It was true. My own family had been getting smaller, shrinking rather than growing. Was it just the fragment of a family now? "I'd like to be part of a real family again," I said wistfully.

"You could be," Jantu said. "And so could I."

"How?"

"You'll see. Watch," Jantu said. She started molding her clay buffalo again. With small twisting movements, her hands teased out four legs, then shaped a pair of horns. Deftly she smoothed and rounded the shape until it had become a miniature water buffalo.

Then, with a flourish, she lifted up a layer of straw in a corner of our shelter. Nestled in the straw was a group of other clay figures. Carefully she set the miniature buffalo next to them. "There," she said. "They're finished—the whole set of them."

"What are they?" I asked. "Can I see?"

Jantu smiled at me mysteriously. "I didn't want to show you until they were all ready."

"And are they ready?"

"They are!" Ceremoniously, Jantu took a clay doll and set it on the stone beam. Just then a few drops of rain started to fall.

Jantu parted a section of the palm frond and scanned the sky anxiously. Thick gray clouds had drifted across to block out the sun. In the distance, a clap of thunder sounded.

The wind picked up and was sweeping up eddies of dust into the air. Then the rain started in earnest, one of those sudden thunderstorms hinting of the monsoons due to come soon. Jantu stretched her sarong protectively over the pile of straw where her clay figures were. Hunched over them like that, she looked like a scruffy hen trying to hatch her precious eggs.

I huddled close to Jantu and listened to the rain drumming on the leaves. Raindrops pierced through the cracks of the palm fronds and felt light and cool on my bare arms. I thought of the long rainy afternoons I had spent on the porch at home when I was very young.

As light and cool as the rain, my grandmother's fingers would massage my scalp while I rested my head in her lap. Nearby, the murmur of my family surrounded me, like a soft blanket.

I closed my eyes now and tried to imagine them all sitting around me: Grandmother stroking me, Father and Sarun whittling on the steps, Mother stoking the embers of the cooking fire. It wasn't just the thick thatched roof that had sheltered me, I realized now. It was the feeling I had had then, of being part of a family as a gently pulsing whole, so natural it was like the breathing of a sleeping baby.

When I opened my eyes, I saw that Jantu had a lost, faraway look in her eyes, and I knew that she was remembering, too, what it was like when her own family was whole and complete.

As the rain died down, Jantu turned to me and smiled. "You still want to play with my family of dolls?" she asked.

I'd rather have my own family back, I thought, but dolls were better than nothing. "Sure," I said.

"Wait, let's set things up for them first," Jantu said. She pointed to the puddle next to the stone beam. "That," she announced, "is the lake. The Tonle Sap lake."

It didn't look very impressive, but I knew Jantu well enough to realize that her tone of voice promised something more. So I waited.

"And this is our village, by the edge of the lake," Jantu said, sticking a tuft of weeds near the puddle.

She rummaged in the pile of straw by the stone beam and took out a small clay doll, about the size of her palm. "Now, this," she said, "is my cousin Nea." It was a lovely doll, with rice grains for eyes, and bits of black string for hair. It even had a scrap of red cloth draped around it for a sarong.

I looked more carefully at that doll. Not only was its sarong the same color as Nea's, but the way its one tiny clay arm rested on its hip, and the slight tilt of its head, reminded me of Nea.

"It looks like her," I said.

Jantu smiled, and set the dainty clay doll next to the tuft of weeds. "That's Nea at home," she explained. Then she took out two other dolls from the straw, one taller and the other smaller than the Nea doll. She held both out to me. "Who do you think these are?" she asked me.

Immediately I recognized Nea's grandfather, because that doll was holding on to a delicate wooden hoe. And the other doll was clearly

Jantu herself, complete with a tiny clay baby hitched up on her hip.

"Grandpa Kem and you," I answered, with growing interest. "What about my family?"

"Right here!" With a flourish, Jantu pulled away the last layer of straw from the pile and revealed a miniature village, with a thatched farmhouse on stilts, oxcarts, a water buffalo, and three more clay figures. I saw that the two larger dolls were my mother and Sarun, and I had no trouble recognizing myself in the last doll.

"My hair isn't that messy," I complained.

Obligingly Jantu smoothed some of the black thread away from the doll's eyes and handed the doll over to me. "How's that?" she said. "And look, you even have a scarf, see? I saved you the best bit of cloth I had. Go on, you can wrap the scarf around her neck."

That's the nice thing about playing with Jantu, I thought happily, as I took the doll modeled on myself. She lets you join in the game. Carefully I wound the scarf around my doll, before setting it down next to the dolls of Mother and Sarun.

With that frown of concentration which meant she wanted absolute silence, Jantu arranged the dolls so tht the two families were grouped on either side of the "Tonle Sap" puddle. The dolls stared at one another across the water.

"Now what?" I asked, impatient for the game to begin.

Jantu sat back on her heels and studied her arrangement. "Well, it's no use being friends, is it," she said, "when our families are going to go back to separte villages? I could shout myself hoarse by the side of Tonle Sap lake, and you'd never even hear me. But suppose"—and here she reached for the Nea doll with one hand and the Sarun doll with the other—"suppose this happened . . ." Jantu paused and bent over the two dolls. Her fingers were deft and light as she molded the clay. When she had finished, she held up the two dolls for me to see. Their hands were now linked by a dab of clay, so tht it looked as if they were holding hands. "What do you think?"

"You mean, suppose Sarun and Nea got married?" I asked.

Jantu grinned. "Suppose they did?" she said. "Let's see what would happen."

Carefully she set the two dolls down in my village, next to the Mother doll. Then she pointed to the doll of herself, left on the other side of the lake. "What do you think would happen to me then?"

"You'd follow Nea, and come live with us," I said.

Jantu grinned. "Absolutely. Move me, go ahead, pick me up and move me."

Gently I picked up the clay figure of Jantu and her baby brother and moved them across the puddle to join "my" family. Left by himself, Grandpa Kem looked rather forlorn. "What about Grandpa Kem?" I asked.

"He goes, too. Move him, that's right."

I did, and saw that there was quite a clan on my side of the lake now, with Sarun and Nea, Grandpa Kem and Mother, Jantu and her baby brother and myself—all clustered around the thatched house. I liked that.

They looked like a real family.

"We'd need to build another house," I said, "for the newlyweds."

Jantu dipped her hands into the puddle and scooped out a lump of clay. Deftly she shaped it into four walls and put some leaves on top of it for a roof. "There," she said. "What else?"

"How about some more animals?"

"I've already got plenty of those," Jantu said. She rummaged behind another part of the stone beam until she brought out a handful of little chickens and ducks and another water buffalo.

"And trees," I said. "We could plant some mango trees. My father loved mangoes."

Jantu hesitated. For a long moment she was silent. "My father liked mango trees, too," she said at last, and her voice was strange, as if a bit of rice had gotten stuck in her throat. "We had a mango orchard behind our house, at home," Jantu said. "Elephant-tusk mangoes. Sweet and long and smooth." She hugged her knees to her chest. "That's where they killed him, between the mango trees. I saw it. Father put his hands up to his face, just before they shot him, I think because he didn't want me to see him scared."

Had my father been scared, too, I suddenly wondered, when they took him away that night? But it had been dark, and I hadn't seen his face.

Jantu took a deep breath. "No mango trees," she said. "We'll plant lemons and guava and papaya trees instead."

I looked down at the puddle. Now it didn't seem like Tonle Sap lake, and the clay dolls looked sad and misshapen. "I don't want to play anymore," I said.

"Come on," Jantu said firmly. "How can you dream if you don't learn to shut off the thoughts you don't want?" She twisted a twig so cleverly that it really did look like a tiny lemon tree, "Here," she said. "That's where the orchard will be."

"All right," I said, and poked another branch beside it. "And that can be the guava trees."

"We can even make some fruit to hang from the trees," Jantu said, and started to stick beads of clay onto the branches.

Then we made plows for the oxen to pull, and fishnets for the lake, and even a cradle for the baby twins that the Nea and Sarun dolls had.

We were just burying some real rice seeds in the furrows that the Sarun doll had plowed near the lake when I looked up and noticed that the sun was setting. The sky had cleared, and a beam of pale sunlight was shining on the miniature rice fields we had made. I knew that Mother would be calling us for dinner soon.

"Let's finish planting the field," I said.

Jantu nodded and poked a few more rice seeds into the moist soil.

By the time the field was planted, it was almost dark. The Nea doll was sitting near her cradle of babies, and Jantu gently rocked the cradle with one finger. "It's time to sing the children to sleep," she said.

And softly, in a sweet clear voice, Jantu sang a lullaby I had never heard before:

> "When the rain is falling,
>   When the rice is growing,
>   When the day is done,
>   Then my little one, my lovely one,
>   Will come home to sleep—and dream."

As she sang, Jantu's eyes glowed with the twilight reflected in them. There was a long silence when her song ended.

"My mother used to sing that to me when I was little," she finally said.

"Teach it to me," I said.

And so, sitting on the ancient stone beam in the fading light, Jantu taught me the lullaby. I closed my eyes and rocked myself slightly as I sang, and thought of sleeping babies, and full harvests, and a home with a real family.

Chapter 7

THE TOY VILLAGE became the center of our world, and Jantu and I played with it every day. Each time we would add a few more things—a rice barn, rain barrels, a pigsty—and as Jantu shaped them, we would make up more stories about our new lives after we left the Border.

Hard though we tried to immerse ourselves in this make-believe world, we could sense the growing tension in the real world around us. As we played with our clay dolls, I could not help but notice that more and more heavily armed soldiers were appearing in the camp, trying to recruit men. Sometimes they would stop at our campsite and talk to Sarun.

The fighting on the Border was growing more intense, they said. The Vietnamese soldiers inside Cambodia were mobilizing their forces for one last attack as part of their dry-season offensive, so the Khmer Serei resistance scattered along the Border had to recruit more men to counter the Vietnamese attack.

"But I don't want to fight," Sarun would say quietly. "I just want to stay through two or three more distributions to collect enough rice and other supplies. Then I'll take my family home before the monsoons, in time to plant the next rice crop."

What about his duty to his country, the soldiers would argue in soft, wheedling voices. Didn't he care about the sovereignty of his country? Didn't he want to help kick out the Vietnamese invaders, and at the same time keep the ruthless Khmer Rouge army at bay, so that there might be peace and prosperity in Cambodia again?

I listened to all this while playing with my clay dolls. How could people "fight for peace," I wondered. Why couldn't we just go home and grow our rice crops? I didn't care which side won, as long as we were allowed to go on with our lives in the village.

In our small make-believe world, at least, life was simple and easy to understand. There were no soldiers and no war, only people like ourselves quietly getting on with their lives. And so, as the soldiers tried to talk my brother into becoming a soldier, I made the clay Sarun doll plow his tiny rice fields.

Late one morning, shortly after Sarun had returned from the second mass distribution with hoe heads and fishnets, we heard the sounds of gunfire and bombing in the distance. At first I didn't even notice them, until Jantu suddenly lifted her head and listened.

Nearby, Grandpa Kem had stopped hammering on the stakes of the new lean-to he'd been building and was also listening.

"What is it?" Nea called to him from her thatched shelter.

"Hush!" her grandfather said.

I stayed very still and listened, too.

The sound was so faint that I thought it might be the lunch truck backfiring. But then the dull thuds grew louder and lasted longer.

"Bombs," Grandpa Kem said quietly. "They're shelling the border."

It was the quiet, tired way he said it that scared me. As if he had known all along it would happen, and that he couldn't do anything about it. I looked at my mother, whose eyes were wide with fear.

"What do we do?" Mother asked Grandpa Kem.

"Start packing," he said. And without another word, he began putting his tools away.

So it was really happening. Even on the Border, the fighting was going to start again. I watched my mother fold up the sleeping mats and clothes into our oxcart, and Sarun load up some of the new hoe heads he had just been given. Mother was trying to pile in some kindling, as Nea and Grandpa Kem hurriedly loaded up their oxcart with their belongings.

I turned to our miniature village. Two dolls were plowing furrows in the fields, while another mended a fishnet. The latest addition, a baby doll in a hammock strung between the lemon trees, was peacefully asleep. I looked at them for a long moment.

"I'm not going," I said.

Jantu reached for a handful of straw and started to cover up the village. "Come on, Dara," she said. "It's just a toy. We have to go."

"I'm not going."

"We can come back to it later," Jantu said. She tugged at my sarong gently. "Come on."

Around us, people were already starting to move. My mother had her arms full of clothes and was yelling at me, "Leave those silly dolls, right now!"

Jantu and I exchanged a quick look. "We could take them," I said.

"They'd break," Jantu said.

"We can try," I said. "I'll carry them."

Jantu shook her head. "Things that can break," she said slowly, "are not worth taking." She picked up one of the clay dolls, and held it. "It's only what you can bring inside of you that really matters. How do you think I was able to say goodbye to my mother and father?" she asked, so softly that she seemed to be talking more to herself than to me. "When they died, I stored it up—everything I remembered about them, loved about them. That's what I bring with me. They're inside me now. Part of me. Do you know what I'm trying to say?"

I shook my head.

"Think about your own father, Dara. Tell me something about him. Something that makes you happy when you think about it."

As I tried to think, I heard the sound of shells exploding, like distant thunder. "I used to be scared of thunder," I told Jantu. "So Father would always hold me in his lap and cup my ears with his hands." And suddenly I could feel his hands tight against my ears again, strong and warm, shutting out all the noise, so that I was in our own snug, safe world. I looked at Jantu. "I understand now," I said. Gently I took the doll from her and left it on a bed of straw by the stone beam.

Within minutes we were on the move. Mother and Sarun had stashed whatever they could in the cart. With thousands of other refugees, we headed into Thailand, away from the shelling.

I had never seen so many people on the move before. Many of the other refugees had set out on foot, taking nothing but bundles of clothing with them. A few had their belongings strapped onto rusty bicycles, which they wheeled clumsily along. Others had baskets dangling from bamboo shoulder poles, filled with utensils and clothing and even children too young to walk.

Swept up by this current, Grandpa Kem drove his oxcart in front, while my mother, with Nea and Sarun, followed in the cart behind him. Jantu, Baby, and I lagged farther behind the carts. They had offered to take Baby, but Jantu had wanted to hold him.

It was eerie, like a dream. Everyone was quiet. Instead of the usual noises of people arguing and laughing and talking, it was now utterly silent. Occasionally the dull boom of shelling would echo from the distance, but that, and the constant scuffling of feet over the dusty road, was all I could hear.

Somewhere along the way I lost my sandals. My feet were sore and hot, and I was very thirsty. I wanted to sit down in the shade and rest, but everyone else was moving, and so I plodded along, too, putting one tired foot in front of the other.

Once I heard a child crying, her shrill sobs cutting through the silence. Then I saw her—a thin little girl in a tattered dress, clutching a plastic doll by its leg. The doll had only two sockets where the arms should have been, and its long, yellow hair swept a semicircle in the dirt as it was swung to and fro. The girl was wailing for her mother, her voice broken and hoarse. Nobody paid any attention to her.

I stared at her until Jantu pulled me away. "Keep walking, or you'll end up like her—lost!" she said.

"But nobody's helping her. How's she going to find her mother?"

"She isn't," Jantu said.

"What's going to happen to her, then?"

"She'll probably get picked up by some soldiers and locked up in the orphanage they have for refugee kids, where they are forced to become slaves, or something."

"Really?"

"If you don't believe me, just start howling for your mother, and see where you'll get locked up! Now come on!"

Shaken, I stumbled after Jantu, clutching on to her shirt so that I wouldn't lose her in the crowd. Ahead of us I caught a glimpse of my own mother, and felt reassured.

We passed several other children like the little girl with the doll, all of them howling for their parents, all of them bypassed by the hurrying grownups.

Everywhere, too, there were signs of the temporary homes that people had tried to build for themselves at Nong Chan—a hammock strung between two saplings, a neat ring of stones around a cooking fire, salted fish hung out to dry in the sun, a shelter woven from plastic bags and cardboard, now abandoned and looking forlorn.

I thought of the spot we had claimed for ourselves around our oxcart. I had liked the way that our damp sarongs fluttered on the laundry line, and that the embers of the cooking fire flickered within its neat circle of stones at night. I liked propping up our dishes to dry on the wooden rack Sarun had made, and our palmetto-thatched hut, which had become a snug, familiar home for me to curl up in at night.

Now it was gone. I thought of the small world of our clay dolls, and sighed. How senseless it was, to have cared about something so unreal.

We trudged on in the glimmering heat of a blazing afternoon sun. Once in a while I saw jeeps drive past at the edge of the crowd, with Thai soldiers in their olive-green uniforms pointing their guns into the crowd. At first I thought they were trying to stop the stream of people from moving farther into Thai territory, but then I noticed that jeeps were driving slowly behind us as well, as if to shepherd us along. When I asked Jantu about it, she just shrugged. "They want to keep an eye on us. Make sure we're not wandering off into their fields." Across the stubbled fields was a cluster of thatched houses, set amid banana trees and bamboo groves. I even caught a glimpse of a little boy driving a flock of geese home.

So that was what it meant to be a refugee. We were farmers who had been displaced from our old land and yet prevented from settling on any new land. Would we always be on the move, people who not only didn't have a home but weren't allowed to build a new home anywhere?

By midafternoon I was very hungry. I had asked Mother to pack some cold rice in a basket, but there hadn't been any left over from breakfast, and so we had left our campsite without food. Jantu must be hungry, too, I thought.

What would the food truck have served today, I wondered. Stew with chunks of yellow squash and strips of pork? Or cabbage and kale seasoned with fish sauce? Certainly there'd be steaming hot white rice—and plenty of it! My mouth watered.

Just then, as if I had dreamed it into taking shape, I saw the food truck in front of me, parked in the shade of a long, thatched building.

I blinked. It looked abandoned, and therefore strangely neglected, but it was unmistakably the food truck.

"Look!" I said, tugging at Jantu's arm.

Jantu glanced at the truck, but kept walking.

"Wait! Can't you see the pots loaded on the truck?"

"Sure," Jantu said. "So what?"

"The pots could be filled with rice. And stew. Yellow squash stew!"

"We can't stop," Jantu said, but she looked more interested.

"We could take a look. A quick look. There's bound to be some food there. You could feed Baby. Come on, it won't take long."

Jantu hesitated. "All right," she said. "You catch up with your mother and tell her what we're doing."

So I ran ahead, ducking between the baskets and bicycle wheels until I caught up with Mother.

"We'll wait for you," she agreed reluctantly. "But don't take too long."

"I promise!" I called over my shoulder, and ran back to Jantu.

We climbed over the bamboo fence separating the road from the compound where the food truck was parked, and ran in.

In the middle of the compound was a large bamboo shed with a thatched roof. I dashed in. It was an enormous kitchen. There were about fifty huge charcoal stoves lining the side walls of woven bamboo strips, and another thirty even bigger stoves in the middle. Some of the stoves still had nuggets of glowing charcoal in them. The cooks had obviously left in a hurry.

The food truck was backed up right against a ramp next to the front door of the kitchen. It looked as if the pots had just been loaded onto the truck when the shelling began.

Jantu climbed up to the truck itself, and I handed Baby up to her. She lifted the lid of the first pot in the truck and peered inside. I waited breathlessly.

"Nothing!" she cried.

I followed her up the truck and peered inside the second pot. Nothing there either, except a thin layer of burnt rice. I realized with sharp disappointment that the truck must have been unloading dirty pots when the shelling started.

"So much for your yellow squash stew!" Jantu said impatiently. "Now we'll have to run back to catch up with the others!"

Holding her brother firmly against her, she jumped off the tailgate of the truck.

Just then everything exploded.

The blast threw me off balance. I crashed into an empty pot sending it spinning through the air. A shell had landed nearby, ripping apart the thatching of the kitchen roof and setting it on fire. Pieces of thatching collapsed onto the matted bamboo sides of the kitchen underneath. Within seconds the whole shed was in flames.

There were screams everywhere.

Outside the compound, people started to stampede. The stream of refugees had turned into a churning, swirling torrent. Like a river bursting its banks, people fled in every direction, scattering and running into the adjoining fields. The jeeps wove through the confusion, honking uselessly, trying to stem the flow.

I groped my way past the rolling pots and jumped off the truck. My one thought was to find Mother.

Then I saw Jantu.

My friend's arms were streaked with blood. She was sobbing, but she seemed unhurt. She was holding on to her baby brother, rocking him jerkily to and fro. I realized that the blood was spurting from the baby, from his plump little foot, which was twisted at a funny angle.

"He's hurt, help me, he's hurt!" Jantu said, sobbing. Baby was crying, too, howling so hard that he face was turning a purplish blue.

"I'll get help," I said. "Wait for me here." And with the sound of their wails ringing in my ears, I rushed off.

Chapter 8

I CLIMBED BACK OVER THE BAMBOO FENCE. The crowd outside had churned up so much dust that I could barely see to the other side of the road. How would I ever find my family among them? I fought off a wave of panic. Taking a deep breath to calm myself, I plunged into the crowd.

Almost at once I was knocked off my feet by the shoving and pushing. I got up and stumbled on. It seemed crucial to move along, if only to keep from being knocked down.

Before I had taken very many steps, someone jostled me. I grabbed blindly for support and fell, pulling down a boy next to me and tripping the frail old woman behind him as well. Dazed, they both sprawled next to me.

Quickly I got up and tried to help the old woman to her feet. But she only groaned and lay there. Already people were stepping on her sarong, her hair, her hands. Again I tried to pull her into a sitting position, but I couldn't budge her.

Desperately I grabbed at someone's sleeve and begged for help. But I was only brushed aside. The boy beside me was crying.

Finally somebody stopped and looked at us. To my great relief, he took charge.

"I'm bringing your grandmother over to that big tree. She'll be safe there," he said. "You follow me, all right?"

I nodded, and the man bent down and lifted the old woman up. As he carried her away, he shouted back at me, "Bring your brother! You want him trampled to death?" I grabbed the wailing child by the hand and stumbled after them.

There was a big tamarind tree by the side of the road, and when we got to it, I saw that there were at least six other people lying in its shade. Most of them had been wounded by the explosion, and blood still glistened on their skin. But one looked dead, a pale young woman whose eyes were locked in an unseeing gaze at the leaves above.

A man with a red cross on an armband moved among the wounded, rinsing off a cut, murmuring reassuring words. Amazing, I thought,

I've managed to come to the right place for help.

The man carrying the frail old woman gently lowered her onto the ground, in the shade. I noticed that he also had on an armband with a red cross. He patted me gruffly and said, "She'll be okay. Just stay with her, and keep an eye on your brother."

"He's not my brother!" I protested. "But Jantu's brother, he's just a baby, he's hurt, back by the food truck. Please come!"

"All right, let's go," he said. Holding my hand, he led me out of the shade of the tamarind tree and back into the crowd.

It was like wading upstream against a strong current, to push against all the people rushing past the other way. I clung to the stranger's hand, and together we plowed our way back to the compound where the food truck was.

There Jantu was huddled against the wheel of the truck, holding her brother. For an awful moment I thought he was dead. But then the baby whimpered softly, and Jantu saw us.

"Over here," she called.

Without a word the man walked over and scooped the baby up in his arms. Then, turning briefly to make sure we were following him, he headed back toward the spreading tamarind tree.

He laid Baby down in the shade, next to the old grandmother. Jantu sat down cross-legged and cradled her brother's head in the lap of her sarong. "Thanks, Dara," she said faintly. "Thanks so much."

"You should thank him," I said, looking up at the stranger who had helped us.

He was examining Baby, rinsing off the blood from his hurt foot. It did not look nearly as bad when it was clean. There was a wide gash where the shard had sliced off some skin, but the cut itself didn't seem to go very deep.

"Will he be all right?" Jantu asked.

"His ankle might be fractured, but don't worry," the man said. "The ambulance should be along soon. They'll have medicine and bandages to treat the wound properly."

Soon a white truck with a big red cross painted on its side arrived, and parked next to the tamarind tree. Four men jumped out and quickly started examining each patient. One of them, a white foreigner with a bushy red beard, came to Jantu's baby brother and murmured something to the baby which we couldn't understand, but which sounded soothing. He examined the ankle, then called a Cambodian nurse over. They talked briefly before the nurse turned to Jantu.

"He says the child has to be hospitalized," the nurse translated. "They'll take him to the hospital inside the Khao I Dang refugee camp, where they can set the bone and watch him for a few days. It's not far from here."

"A few days?" Jantu echoed in dismay. "But he can't be alone that long! He's only a little—"

"Of course you'd have to go along with him, child." She glanced at us. "Unless you have a parent or older relative to accompany him?"

Jantu hesitated. "I . . . I don't. I mean, I do, but I've got to find them first. You see, just now when the bombing . . ."

But even as Jantu was talking, the red-bearded doctor had picked up her brother and was carrying him into the white van. Jantu ran up to him, pulling at his sleeve to protest. He ignored her. Quickly he laid the baby down on a mattress on the floor of the van and gestured for Jantu to climb in next to the baby.

She turned to me in desperation. "What are we going to do?" she asked. She looked scared and confused.

"I don't know," I said. I felt every bit as scared as Jantu looked. "I guess you'll just have to go along with Baby."

"What about you?" Jantu asked.

"I . . . I'll come with you."

Jantu shook her head. "No, Dara, you've got to stay," she said. "You've got to find our families and tell them Baby's hurt, and in the hospital with me."

"They know where the hospital is," I argued. "Let them find us there."

"They won't look there, Dara. Don't you see, they'll just think we're lost."

There, it was out.

Lost: that single, terrifying word. I felt as if a rock had slammed against my stomach and lodged there. I had been thinking of it all this time, but was afraid to bring it up. Now Jantu had said it. We were lost. Just like that little girl with the broken doll, crying in the crowd. For a second I felt like wailing for Mother, too.

"You have to find them," Jantu said grimly.

I started at her. "How?" I demanded.

"They'll be around." Jantu would not look at me. "Someone will be there."

"Where?"

"Nearby. Somewhere."

"But where? Where? Tell me where?" My voice shook.

"By the stone beam," Jantu said firmly, with some of her old authority. "They're bound to go back to our old campsite to wait for us. So just find your way back to our campsite, Dara. You can do it."

I shook my head. "No," I said. "I can't."

"You have to, Dara. It's the only way to link up with them again. And you know where our stone beam is. By the well, Dara."

"Which well? There're hundreds of wells like ours. How can I find the right one?" I was beginning to sound shrill, but I couldn't help it.

"You'll find it, Dara. And when you do, your mother and Sarun and Nea and Grandpa Kem—they will all be there, waiting."

"How do you know that?" I asked. "Suppose I can't find the stone beam? Suppose there's nobody waiting there for me?" I swallowed hard, trying to fight a mounting panic.

"You've got to try, Dara."

I took a look around. People were swirling past, like waves in a churning human sea. Thousands of faces, and not one that looked familiar.

With a stab of longing I suddenly thought of home—not of our makeshift shelter somewhere at the Border, but of my real home. I thought of Grandmother's little herb garden of basil and turmeric and lemon grass, soaking up the morning sunshine under her kitchen window.

"Oh, Jantu," I said, "I'm scared."

For a moment Jantu did not speak. Picking up a lump of mud, she kneaded it in one hand. "Of course you're scared," she said slowly. "It's a scary world out there. But we're here, and we're stuck with it, aren't we?" She started to roll the lump of clay in her hands. Her voice was as calm and rhythmic as the movement of her fingers, kneading the clay, shaping it. "We've got to do the best we can, out of what we've got," she said.

I watched Jantu's long fingers, her hands lightly cupping the clay, circling each other in a kind of fluid dance. And as I watched, the clay took shape, becoming rounder and smoother, smoother and glossier.

"Remember that marble I made after Chnay smashed my rice-husking dolls? I told you it was a magic marble."

I nodded, remembering how just holding that smooth, round marble had made me feel better.

"Did you believe me? Did you think it was a magic marble?" Jantu asked.

Again I nodded.

Jantu smiled. She continued to roll the ball of clay in her hands, sculpting it, rounding it. "I'm making you another marble, Dara," she said. "Except this one will be more powerful. It will have stronger magic in it." Her fingers stopped moving, and she opened her hand. Cupped in one palm was a perfectly round, perfectly smooth clay marble.

I reached out and took the marble from Jantu's hand. It was still moist and felt solid and heavy. Just moments before, it had been a lump of mud in a dirty puddle. Now Jantu had shaped it into a perfect sphere.

"Is it really a magic marble?" I asked.

Solemnly Jantu nodded. "It will make you strong, and brave, and patient," she said.

"But will it help me find my mother?"

Jantu took a deep breath. "If you believe in it, it will help you," she said. She reached out and closed my fingers over the marble. "Now go," she said.

The sun was already low on the horizon, and a light breeze had sprung up. The shelling had stopped, and in the quiet I could hear skylarks singing in the fields. I took a last look at Jantu and the baby.

Then I turned away and started walking east, away from the safety of Thailand. My shadow stretched out long and thin in front of me. It would be dark before too long, I thought, but I would not be afraid. The magic marble was firm and smooth in my hand.

Chapter 9

I KEPT WALKING even after the sun had set. The sky was still tinged with gold, but I knew that soon everything would be swallowed up in darkness and I would have to stop searching for my family.

I had managed to retrace part of the way we had come earlier that afternoon, but I was nowhere near where our campsite had been. In the fading light I could make out the silhouettes of all the tall watchtowers in the distance rising on their bamboo stilts above the desolate plains. I kept heading toward them, since they marked where the Nong Chan camp officially began.

It was already dark when I reached the watchtowers. Scattered campfires had been lit near them, as if other people found it reassuring to be sheltering near these landmarks. Families gathered quietly around the fires, sorting out their belongings, or bedding down for the night. Many others had not even bothered to build a fire, but were just huddled on the ground, sleeping under the open sky.

For a while I wandered from fire to fire, searching the faces of the people reflected in the firelight for someone I knew. But there was not a familiar face among them.

I noticed an old man looking at me curiously. He was sitting with his own family, holding a plate of cold rice. I looked at it hungrily, but could not bring myself to ask for any food. The old man smiled at me kindly.

Ask him, I told myself. If not for food, at least for some directions. I took a step toward him, then hesitated. What would I ask?

I wondered what Mother was doing now. Of course, she would be worried about me, I thought, but at least she would be with Sarun and Nea and Grandpa Kem. I imagined her stoking the embers of a cooking fire, at that very moment thinking of me. And perhaps Grandpa Kem, Sarun, and Nea would be sitting nearby, staring silently into the flames. Just imagining them all made me feel lonely. On the twilight horizon, a crescent moon was rising. I watched it hook on to a branch right above me, and dangle there, like a new sickle blade gleaming in the darkening sky.

If only I could climb up this tree to the moon, I thought drowsily, and curl up against its smooth curve, how comfortable I'd be tonight. Or I could hang on to it as it swept across the night sky, and search down far below for my mother.

Tomorrow, I promised myself, I will go on looking. Tomorrow I will find them. For now, the tree in front of me looked old and solid. I leaned against it, pressing my cheek against its rough bark. It seemed as good a place as any to rest. So I lay down under it and felt for Jantu's marble in my shirt pocket. It was there, smooth and round, reassuring. I took it out and, with it in my hand, fell asleep.

It was dawn when I woke up. A cool morning breeze was blowing, and I shivered, rubbing the goose bumps from my bare arms. Then I got up and stretched.

I was cold and hungry, but I felt a certain pride that I had survived the night alone, with only the clay marble for company. Maybe Jantu's magic was working, I thought. Maybe the magic in the marble is making me stronger and more sure of myself. Quickly I checked my pocket to make sure I had put it back, and then, taking a deep breath, I started to walk on again.

Already there were people up and about, many of them packing their bundles of clothes, ready to move on. I picked my way through them. I felt as if I were just about invisible, for all the attention anyone was paying me. I heard a group of men talking about the shelling yesterday, and I lingered there, eavesdropping on their conversation.

What I heard was disturbing. The shelling was expected to start again, someone said, except that today it might be coming from the other direction: from the west and aimed at the east. Would that be Thailand shooting back at the Vietnamese, or perhaps the various anti-Vietnamese Khmer factions shooting at each other?

The men discussed this at length, but nobody seemed to have any clearer sense of what to do than I did. What everyone did seem convinced about was that the fields here at Nong Chan would be unsafe for at least the next few days—maybe longer—and that we should seek shelter elsewhere. But where? Some talked about walking back into Thailand, perhaps toward the protected, more established refugee camps, like Khao I Dang. Others talked of joining one of the military base camps scattered deep in the forests beyond Nong Chan.

Listening to all this, I felt a stab of fear. If I didn't find the stone beam, it would be even harder to meet up with my family, as the continued shelling would scatter us yet farther apart. I had to find them, and soon.

But how?

I noticed that the kind old man who had smiled at me the night before was among the group of men I had just been listening to. Sitting a little off to the side, he was eating some cold rice out of a small woven basket. Slowly I approached him. He looked up at me and beckoned for me to come over.

"Where's your family, child?" he asked.

"I . . . I don't know," I said.

He shook his head sadly. "Got separated from them during the shelling yesterday, did you? I thought so. Look, I don't have much rice left. Take this." He held out the last bit of rice in his basket to me and said, "If you're hungry, why don't you try waiting for the lunch truck?"

Of course, the lunch truck! Why hadn't I thought of that before? The lunch truck was one of the very few things around that had its own set routine and destinations. People—especially children— would know where it stopped. I could ask for directions to the signpost with the red "3" painted on it. From there I could easily find my way back to the stone beam!

"Thank you," I said to the old man, taking the handful of sticky rice. And as I turned away, I also silently thanked the magic marble, for showing me the way.

People were still in a state of flux, looking for their old campsites or for someplace safer. I asked the first child I saw for directions to the lunch truck stop, and got them. I started walking, continuing to ask children along the way for further directions. By early afternoon I had managed to find my way to the truck stop where Jantu and I had so often lined up for our lunch.

The wooden signpost with the red "3" was still standing, although there wasn't a single child waiting at it.

I barely paused there. Everything was starting to look familiar. Almost running, I headed past the well. Forgotten were my hunger and my sore feet. I wanted only to get home and throw myself into Mother's waiting arms. Should I slow down, and creep up to surprise Mother and Sarun? Or should I just keep running, and shout to get their attention? I could hardly keep from laughing out loud as I ran the last stretch home.

Suddenly I stopped.

There was nothing there.

The flat landscape stretched out, bleak and familiar. But there was no oxcart parked there, no laundry flapping nearby, no hammock strung under it. There was no campfire, no tarpaulin sheet draped over bags of rice and tools.

And there was no one from my family.

They must be nearby, I thought. Desperately I tried to find Mother or Sarun in the scattered crowd of people.

A mistake, I thought. I must have made a mistake again. I was at the wrong spot after all. I would just have to keep looking further. I glanced around, trying to get my bearings.

It was then that I saw our old stone beam half jutting out of the mud and, to one side of it, our toy village.

Or what was left of it.

The puddle that Jantu and I had pretended was Tonle Sap lake was still there, but the houses were gone, trampled into the mud. I walked over to the puddle and knelt down. From the mud I pulled up a twig that I recognized as our lemon tree. The tiny clay beads that we had hung on it had dissolved, and the twig itself was broken. I tried to stick it back into the mud, but it wouldn't stand.

Fragments of the dolls, now only bits of hardened clay, were scattered nearby. I crouched over the broken clay dolls and tried to piece a few of them together, but I couldn't even tell which pieces were part of which dolls anymore. There was a scrap of cloth that had been the Nea doll's sarong, and a pair of tiny clasped hands that had linked the Sarun doll to the Nea doll, but nothing else was even recognizable.

I laid my cheek down on the sun-warmed stone and pressed against the carved pattern on it. The carving on this one stone has survived a thousand years, I told myself. What does it matter that your silly clay dolls didn't make it through the night? I closed my eyes, but the tears trickled out just the same, until my cheeks were cool and slippery against the stone.

Chapter 10

W<small>HAT ARE YOU CRYING ABOUT?</small> Those stupid clay toys?"

Wiping my cheeks hastily, I looked up. It was Chnay, the bully who had once smashed Jantu's delicate mobile.

I swallowed hard and tossed the clay fragments into the puddle. For a moment, ripples webbed the surface, then disappeared. I stood up and faced Chnay. "You broke our clay dolls," I said.

"Not this time." Chnay grinned. "I know who did, though."

I looked at the flattened village and tried to shrug. "I don't care," I said.

"It was your brother," Chnay said.

"Sarun did that?" I did not believe it.

Chnay pointed at the ruts running through the toy village.

"You see those cartwheel tracks? They're his."

"You saw Sarun drive off?" I asked. "And my mother?"

"What's the matter? Did you really expect them to sit around here waiting for you to show up?" Chnay laughed.

I knew he was mocking me, but I swallowed my pride and asked again if he had really seen them go off.

"Sure," Chnay said.

"When?"

"When what?"

"When did they drive off?"

"Well, it wasn't as simple as that," Chnay said slowly, as if he was savoring my impatience. "They were here early this morning, all waiting around. They seemed to be very worried. Your mother was crying, and I heard her say she wanted to go look for you, but the others restrained her." He looked at me curiously. "What happened to you, anyway? Got separated and lost?"

I nodded impatiently, and told him how Jantu's baby brother had gotten hurt. "Then what?" I asked. "How come they aren't here now?"

"I'm coming to that," Chnay said slowly, clearly enjoying his power. "Well, this band of soldiers came by, armed with AK-47s and grenade launchers."

"What about the soldiers?"

"They started telling your brother how dangerous it'd be staying out in the open, and how he should move his family and supplies to their base camp, where the military would protect them."

"And so they left?" I asked. "All of them?"

"Well, your mother wanted to stay and wait for you, but Sarun insisted that she leave. Said the family shouldn't be split up any further."

I felt a sick, sinking feeling in my stomach. Abandoned: I bit down on my lips, very hard, to stop the tears from welling up. It had been so hard just to find the stone beam. How could I ever hope to find my family now that they had left the only landmark I knew? I looked around, past the people milling in the surrounding field, to the forest beyond. It seemed hopeless.

"Your mother was crying very hard," Chnay added helpfully.

"She'll be back," I said with a confidence I did not feel. "I'll just wait here for her."

"Didn't you just hear me? They decided it's too dangerous to stay out here in the open. Even if you stay here, they aren't going to come back for you. At least not for a while. You'd be better off going after them."

Reluctantly I considered this. I didn't like the idea of going off on my own again, but it did sound like a sensible thing to do.

"Where did they go?" I asked Chnay.

He pointed to the southeast. "See that rutted trail which leads out from the fields into the forest beyond it? They took that trail. Took all their precious rice supplies, both oxcarts, everything."

"Where does that trail lead?" I asked. "Aren't there several base camps out there? Which one did they go to?"

Chnay shrugged. "How would I know?" he said.

"Didn't they tell you?"

"Tell me?" Chnay laughed. "Who'd tell me anything? Nobody even sees me."

I looked at him. His hair was matted and unkempt, and all the buttons but one on his shirt were missing. For the first time I felt sorry for him, now that I had a taste of what it was like to be totally ignored, to feel unwanted. I could imagine him standing on the side, watching silently as my family bustled about, fretting, discussing, making decisions.

"So you really have no idea where they are?" I asked.

"I didn't say that. What I said was that nobody ever tells me anything. That doesn't mean I don't find out things for myself." He smiled smugly at me. There was a military base camp east of Nong Chan, he told me, where a large group of Khmer Serei soldiers lived. "Their leader is a man called General Kung Silor," Chnay said. "And he's actively recruiting men to join his army, to prepare a counter-attack against the Vietnamese. If men join up now, he'll take them in, feed them and clothe them, and provide some shelter for their families." After the shelling yesterday, Chnay said, a lot of people apparently felt Nong Chan wasn't safe enough anymore, so hundreds of them had decided to join up with Kung's army and move their families over to the security of the base camp there.

"And that's where my family and Jantu's are now? At this base camp?"

That's where I think they are," Chnay hedged.

"But you're not sure?"

He tilted his chin up belligerently. "Who can be sure of anything?" he said.

I felt very tired. My knees gave way, and I sat down heavily on the ground. I had no idea what to do next.

Chnay glanced at me, then rummaged in his pockets. He brought out a handful of cold rice wrapped in a strip of banana leaf. "Here, take it," he said, squatting beside me.

I looked at it hungrily.

"I can always get more," Chnay said, his hand outstretched.

I took it. I crammed a chunk of rice into my mouth and chewed. There was even some fish sauce flavor on it. I smiled, and Chnay smiled back at me. Why, he doesn't look mean at all when he smiles, I thought.

When I had finished his rice, I felt quite a bit better. "How far away is this base camp?" I asked.

"About three miles," Chnay said. "Through the forest." He squinted at the sun, then pointed slightly away from it.

"How long would it take to get there?"

"You should reach it long before nightfall."

"And the trails through the forest, are they well marked?"

"Should be. Besides, there'll be a lot of people heading that way. Just find someone who's going to join Kung Silor's army, and follow him."

"You make it sound so easy."

He shrugged. "Nothing to it."

I got up and dusted off my sarong. "Well, I guess I'll start off," I said. I took a few steps, then paused. "Thanks for the rice," I added.

"It's all right," he said. He was still squatting on the ground, hugging his knees to his chest. He looked small and forlorn.

I waved at him, and walked a few more steps.

There were people everywhere, but not a single one looked familiar, or paid any attention to me. I felt very alone. If I disappeared into thin air right now, I thought, nobody would even realize it. Except maybe Chnay.

I turned and looked back at him.

"Hey!" I called.

He was looking at me sideways, with one cheek resting on his drawn-up knees. "What do you want now?" he asked.

I took a deep breath. "Do you want to come along?"

For a moment he frowned, as if he didn't know what to make of this. Then his face brightened.

"Sure, why not?" he said, and grinned.

He got up, and together we started walking toward the forest.

Chapter 11

THE PATH WOUND THROUGH THE EDGE of the Nong Chan plain, and into the forest behind it. Everyone seemed to know where Kung Silor's camp was, so asking for directions was no problem, especially when we met up with some newly recruited soldiers who were on the way to the base camp themselves.

Still, it was a long walk. My bare feet, which had been sore from all the walking the day before, were tougher now. Perhaps they would soon be like Chnay's, I thought, so thick and callused that they wouldn't feel anything. For now, though, I still missed my sandals.

Just as I was about to suggest a rest, I noticed that the thickets of trees and bamboo groves had thinned out, and in the distance there was a clearing.

We could hear the sound of men singing, and cautiously we made our way closer. From behind some thick bushes we watched as rows of men, all carrying rifles, marched across the square of tamped-down earth. Following the loud commands of an officer, they paced up and down, sharply turning left or right at his every order. Then they lined up in the center of the square and faced the flagpole there. Starkly silhouetted against the twilight sky was the blue-and-white Khmer Serei flag. At a signal, they all saluted the flag, and started singing a strident song with words like "liberation" and "freedom" mixed with "blood" and "death."

"That's the national anthem for the Khmer Serei," Chnay whispered in my ear.

"Well, I don't like it," I whispered back. Perhaps it was the lengthening shadows, or the presence of all those soldiers bristling with weapons, but I felt uneasy and scared.

Chnay led the way down a path that veered off from the square farther into the camp. We paused at a narrow wooden bridge that spanned a deep trench stretching along one side of the square. There were bamboo spikes on the bottom of the trench. I shivered.

"What do we do now? Do we start looking for my family?" I asked.

Chnay seemed uncertain and subdued. "I'm not sure," he said.

I looked around at the gathering dusk with deep misgivings. What were we doing in the middle of the dark forest, I wondered, with nowhere to go and nothing to eat?

As if sensing my thoughts, Chnay pointed to an abandoned lean-to with torn thatching for a roof, and suggested that we sleep there. Without waiting for my answer, he crawled into the shelter and curled up in the corner. As I hesitated outside, he beckoned me in impatiently. "Get some sleep," he said. "We'll look for your family tomorrow."

We? So Chnay was going to help me look for my family? I realized then that I had made a friend, and quietly crept under the thatching and lay down next to Chnay.

I spent a restless night, tossing about listening to the torn thatching flapping in the wind. The forest sounded strange and scary, alive with the grunts and shuffling of mysterious animals. I scrunched up into a small ball and waited for the morning.

At some point I must have dozed off, because when I opened my eyes, Chnay was standing over me, grinning. "Breakfast," he announced and, squatting next to me, held out some cold rice on a banana leaf.

"Where did you get it?" I asked.

"I took it," he said.

"What do you mean? Who did you take it from?"

Chnay looked annoyed. "Do you want it or not? If you're going to be so picky about where your food comes from, I can eat it up by myself."

"You stole it," I said.

With a defiant tilt of his chin, Chnay started eating the rice. "Not really," he said. "It's a kind of secret sharing, that's all. I just don't bother to tell the people that they're sharing their things with me. Anyway, food's meant to be eaten by the hungry."

I was about to protest when my stomach rumbled. Chnay was right, I thought. Food was meant to be shared. I reached out and broke off a chunk of the rice for myself.

That day, Chnay and I wandered around at the base camp, looking for my family. It was hard to know where to begin. If Chnay had not been with me, I would probably have been too timid and scared to do much more than huddle in a corner somewhere by myself. With his guidance, though, we began by slowly circling the outer edges of the sprawling base camp, where hundreds of new families had come for shelter.

It took the better part of the day just to circle the camp once, and by nightfall I was tired and very hungry. That night we returned to the spot where we had slept before and went to sleep with empty stomachs. I missed my mother terribly. It seemed so lonely to come back someplace and not have anybody to even ask you where you had been. Slipping my hand into my pocket, I rubbed the magic marble Jantu had given me. I knew that Chnay would only laugh if he knew about it, but as I drifted off to sleep, I held the marble in my hand and silently asked it to help me find my mother.

The next day we continued our search making a smaller circle inside the first one, but again there was no sign of my family. The disheartening thing about looking was knowing that more families were coming in every day, as the shelling and fighting outside the camp had picked up again. And I couldn't go back to the stone beam to check if anyone was waiting for me there, since it was now too dangerous to walk back to the open fields at Nong Chan.

The only thing I could do was to wander around the military base camp, peering into the faces of every person I saw. I was surprised how I could slip in among groups of people and look at them without their taking the slightest notice of me. But as I began to know my way around the base camp. I began to enjoy being unnoticed. It meant I could be wherever I wanted, whenever I wanted.

I was also learning how to scrounge for food on my own. Unlike Chnay, I never actually stole food, but I found that if I edged up close to a family at their mealtime and stared, refusing to budge even if they tried to wave me off, they might offer me a scrap of food just to make me go away. Still, the handouts were never very substantial, and, more often than not, I would go to sleep hungry.

Late afternoon of the fourth day, Chnay and I had completed our sixth and smallest circle around the camp and had still found no sign of my family. The only area we hadn't yet covered was the military headquarters next to the big square where we had seen the soldiers saluting their flag that first evening.

"What do we do now?" I asked Chnay.

Chnay surveyed the area around us. Clustered around the square were a dozen thatched huts, the biggest of which was, Chnay told me, where General Kung Silor himself lived. Behind them were tents for higher-ranking officers, and nearby were the long thatched barracks for the enlisted soldiers.

"We could look around the barracks," Chnay said without enthusiasm.

"What's the use?" I said, on the verge of tears. "They won't be there." I was tired and discouraged and hungry, and everything seemed bleak. How could I ever hope to find my family when I didn't have the energy to go on looking for them?

It was then that I smelled it—something so wonderful that I was suddenly alert. Roast chicken: my nose was never wrong. My brother had often teased me about it, saying that I could sniff out ripening tamarind pods or guava fruit before even the bees got to them. I sniffed the air now and knew that it was roasting chicken.

The smell was coming from the cluster of thatched huts across the ditch, where the kitchen for the officers must be. I nudged Chnay. "Let's go take a look, over there," I said.

Quickly we made our way across the square to the cluster of huts. The smell of the chicken was stronger, and I was sure it came from a long thatched building near a large tent.

As we passed this tent, I saw a group of men sitting inside, on a platform built of split bamboo, their rifles leaning against them. At their center was a bare-chested man who seemed to be doing most of the talking, his voice a low, deep murmur. Gleaming against his brown chest was a large white crescent dangling from a gold chain that glinted in the late afternoon sun. As I stared at it, the man glanced up and saw me. He frowned, as if about to say something, but Chnay tugged at me, and I walked past.

We approached the kitchen and peered into the doorway. It was dim inside, and except for the flickering light cast by the charcoal fires, the long room was in shadow. Moving among the shadows were some people fanning the charcoal fires. And roasting over the glowing embers were rows of skewered chicken, the skin a glistening golden brown.

My mouth watered. I could almost taste the tender meat as I imagined biting into a piece, tearing at the crispy skin.

I glanced at Chnay. Without a word, the two of us crept closer. There was no one outside, and the doorway was unguarded, except for a little furry monkey chained to the doorpost.

Motioning for me to stay by the doorway, Chnay tried to slip in. The monkey bared its fangs at him and shuffled forward, dragging its chain noisily behind it. Chnay eyed it warily.

I saw a bunch of bananas hanging on the other side of the door, out of the monkey's reach. Quickly I twisted one off and tossed it at the monkey. It hesitated, then snatched at the banana, and Chnay was able to slip past. Keeping as close to the wall as he could. Chnay inched his way toward the closest row of chickens.

As I watched, my heart pounding, he darted out of the shadows and tore a drumstick off a roasting chicken. He looked around, saw that no one had noticed him, and quickly tore off another one. Then, flashing me a triumphant grin, he sprinted to the door.

I had been so engrossed in watching him that I hadn't seen the monkey finish its banana and dart back to the doorway. When Chnay ran out the door, it suddenly lunged out, screeching.

Startled, Chnay kicked at it, but missed. Yammering furiously, the monkey hurled itself at Chnay, snarling and baring its pointed white teeth. It might well have bitten Chnay had the metal chain around its neck not pulled it short, just inches away from his ankles.

Alerted by the sound, one of the cooks rushed out of the kitchen and grabbed Chnay's arm. Chnay struggled, trying to twist free, as the cook yelled for help.

From the other direction, the tall bare-chested man appeared. "What's going on?" he demanded.

Scared, I tried to run past him, but he caught me by the wrist.

"Who are you?" he growled, bending down to look at me. The white crescent-shaped object dangling from his chain, I saw now, was a huge tiger's tooth. He shook me by the arm, roughly. "What're you up to?" he asked.

I opened my mouth, but no sound came out.

"They were trying to steal food, sir," the cook said, still hanging on to Chnay.

"Stealing food? How dare they steal from Kung Silor?" the man with the tiger tooth demanded.

I swallowed hard. So this was the leader of the base camp. We couldn't have gotten into worse trouble if we had tried.

"Well? Answer me!" he thundered.

I could tell by the stricken look on Chnay's face that he wasn't going to be any help. I slipped my free hand into my pocket and took out my magic marble. Please, I begged it silently, please give me courage. Make me strong, and brave. The marble felt heavy and smooth in my fist, and as I held it, I felt it radiate a kind of power. I took a deep breath, and felt calmer. "I'm sorry, Mr. Kung, sir," I managed to say. "But we were hungry."

"That doesn't mean you can steal my food," Kung Silor said sternly.

Well, how else would we have gotten it, I thought. To my horror, I found that I had spoken the thought aloud. Was that the magic marble at work?

Kung Silor looked taken aback, then amused. "You could have asked for it," he said.

I looked at the drumsticks in Chnay's hand. A trickle of oil dripped off them. At that moment I felt I wanted a piece of chicken more badly than I have ever wanted anything. Impulsively, I took one of the drumsticks from Chnay, then turned to Kung Silor. "Fine, I'll ask for it, then. Can I have it, please?" I said.

The cook gasped. "Insolent brat!" he hissed, and made a move to grab me.

Kung Silor waved him aside. He studied me with new interest. "I like you, little girl," he said. "You've got spirit."

"My name's Dara," I told him. "And I'm not little."

"All right, Dara, I'll let you off this time. But don't let me catch you stealing any more food, or I'll have your mother whip you."

"Yes, sir," I said. My instincts told me not to reveal that I didn't know where my mother or any of my family were.

He started to turn away, dismissing us all with an absentminded wave.

"Sir," I called out, "about that piece of chicken . . ."

"Yes, yes," he said impatiently. "Take it."

"Thank you, sir," I said. "But could we have some rice with it, too, please?"

He laughed, a deep throaty sound. "Anything else you want, Dara?" he said.

I squeezed the marble for good luck. "I'd like to work in the kitchen," I said quickly. "In exchange for free meals."

Kung Silor looked at the cook. "Well, could you use her? How about it?"

The cook glared at me. "If you say so, sir," he said reluctantly. He released Chnay and stalked back into the kitchen.

When we were left to ourselves again, Chnay looked at me with something close to awe.

"Kung Silor is right," he said. "You've got spirit."

I smiled, but I knew it was actually the magic that Jantu had put in the marble.

Chapter 12

THE NEXT DAY I was kept busy in the kitchen with chores assigned me by the cook. All morning I scrubbed pots so thickly encrusted with soot that my arms were aching long before I was through. Then, after a brief break for lunch, I was told to peel a huge basket piled high with garlic. Only when dinner was quietly simmering on the rows of stoves did I have a quiet moment to myself.

Taking the place of rice and stew the cook had ladled out for me, I retreated to a corner of the kitchen where the cook had had me sleep the night before. Chnay had promised me that he would spend the day looking around for my family, and I had been waiting impatiently for him to bring me news. But there had been no sign of him.

I had finished almost all the rice on my plate before I noticed that the monkey was watching me, its bright, black-rimmed eyes unblinking. Taking a handful of rice, I offered it to the monkey. It did not move.

"Well, go on, take it," I said. "I won't hurt you if you won't hurt me." I tossed the rice at the monkey. It edged forward, its chain clinking behind it, and snatched up the lump of rice, skittering back into the shadows before eating.

I laughed. "You know, I don't mind what you did to us last night," I said, glad to have somebody to talk to. "In fact, I guess I should be grateful. Otherwise I wouldn't be eating so well." The monkey cocked its head, as if listening intently.

"I haven't had much to eat for days now," I said. "You know how it is. If you don't have a family, nobody bothers to feed you." I tossed another lump of rice at the monkey, closer this time. The little monkey came forward and ate it right there, without retreating to its corner.

"I wonder how you lost your family? You look like you need a mother yourself. You're just a baby, really, aren't you?" I had seen how baby monkeys clung on to their mother's fur, as the mothers swung from tree to tree in the forest. "Did you fall off one day, and get lost? Or did some soldiers shoot your mother, and bring you back here?"

It crept even closer, and I held out the last bit of my rice. "Poor thing, you're all alone now, aren't you?" The monkey came up to me and took the rice right from my hand. Its paw was leathery and padded. As it daintily ate the rice, I reached out and stroked its furry wrist.

The shadows lengthened into night, and still Chnay did not come. Only when it was pitch-dark, and the full moon risen high above the tallest sugar palm tree, did he finally show up.

Before he would tell me anything, he nagged me into getting him a plate of leftover rice. I slipped into the kitchen storage room and got some rice and pork rind for him.

"I didn't find them yet, but I think they're definitely here," Chnay said, crunching noisily on his pork rind. "I found out there's a whole other section on the northern edge of the base camp that we never explored. They're probably there."

"So you'll look there tomorrow?" I asked.

"Why should I? They're your family." Chnay scowled, and for a moment he seemed like the mean, tough bully who used to smash our toys.

I hesitated, biting my lips. "Please?" I asked, adding "There will be pork and basil leaf for dinner tomorrow night."

Chnay smiled, and his face softened. "Fine. I'll keep looking if you will keep feeding me," he said.

I considered this for a while, then nodded. "That sounds like a good idea," I said. And then, picking up his empty plate, I went back into the kitchen for another helping of rice for him.

After that, so promptly would Chnay show up for his dinner every night that I suspected he had been waiting in the shadows for some time. I would sneak him out the bowlful of food that I had kept aside, and we would talk as he ate. But he never had any news to report.

On the third evening, I refused to give him any food. "How do I even know you're really searching for them?" I demanded. "You could have just fooled around all day, and then come here for your free dinner."

Chnay took a look at me and turned away. "If that's the way you feel, I might as well leave right now," he said quietly. There was none of the bluff and swagger in his voice that I had seen in him before, only a kind of disappointment. Without another word, he started walking away.

"Wait, don't go!" I said, pulling him back to his usual spot under the palm tree. "I'll get your dinner. What do you want? Cabbage stew or salted fish?"

"Both," he said promptly, and sat down.

"I was at the square all day," Chnay said as he spooned some cabbage into his mouth. "Watching the new recruits practice marching around the flagpole. There are thousands of newly recruited soldiers due to swear allegiance to the Khmer Serei flag. I hear all sorts of ministers and officials have been invited, too, and there'll be a huge banquet after the flag-raising ceremony . . ."

"What do I care about some stupid ceremony," I said. "I want to find my family!"

"That's why I was at the square," Chnay said patiently. "With everybody standing around watching the drills, I thought I might spot your mother there. And I thought if Sarun was one of those recruits, I might spot him, too."

"Well, did you?"

Chnay paused dramatically. "I thought I saw your brother, or somebody who looked like him, marching around the flagpole."

"You thought? Why didn't you make sure?"

"They were all marching by so fast, I couldn't catch up with him, " Chnay said. "But I'll go back tomorrow and look again."

I took a deep breath. "Are you just making this up?" I demanded. "Or do you really think you saw Sarun?"

"I wouldn't lie to you," he said. "Not even for cabbage stew and salted fish every night."

The next day I could not keep my mind on my chores in the kitchen. It took me twice as long to scrub the pots, because I would drift into a daydream about finding my family. And that afternoon the cook had to yell at me three times before I heard him. When I hurried over to him, he was in a foul mood.

"Pay attention," he snapped. "I don't know why I even bother with you, a skinny little orphan like you." He glowered at me.

"I'm not an orphan," I said.

"Well, you're little, and you sure are skinny. But I guess I need all the help I can get. Well, don't just stand there, child. Let's go!" Impatiently he beckoned me to follow him out of the kitchen.

Obediently I trailed after him as he walked out of the kitchen and down a narrow path past Kung Silor's quarters. We crossed the bamboo bridge over the trench. The path widened and then opened out toward the parade grounds.

People were bustling about, hammering planks to make a large wooden platform for a stage. Loudspeakers had been strapped onto the palm trees, and marching songs were being played over the air. Hundreds of women and ragged children stood at the edge of the parade ground, gazing at the soldiers.

Marching in elaborate formations around the flagpole were the soldiers. Dressed in the dappled green of jungle fatigues, they looked deadly serious, each with a gleaming rifle jutting from his shoulder.

Quickly I scanned their faces. They seemed so grim and fierce that I was almost afraid of finding Sarun among them.

"What're you standing there for? Hurry up, I don't have all day!" the cook snapped. He walked on ahead, skirting around the square, toward a path on the opposite side.

"It's hard enough feeding the general and his staff," he grumbled, walking so quickly that I had to run just to keep up with him. "Now I'm supposed to feed the new recruits, too? Just because their rice rations have run out, I have to get more rice for them?"

"Where're we going?" I asked.

He ignored me and kept on walking. I followed him to the opposite side of the square.

It was quieter here, as the spectators seemed to be confined to the other side. The cook veered off and headed toward a low thatched shed that looked as if it had been hastily built. As I approached, I instantly recognized the sound that was coming from this shed: it was rice being pounded. Dum-dedum-dum-dedum. The steady rhythm of wooden poles pounding at mortars of unhusked rice grains was something I had grown up with and always liked. In the midst of this army camp, against the background of marching songs and loud military orders, the pounding sounded reassuringly familiar.

I remembered the clever toy mobile that Jantu had made, with the dolls of two village women pounding rice. Playing with the toy had reminded me of home and made me happy. Now, with the pounding of real rice-husking in that shed, how much closer I felt to home! I looked up at the cook expectantly. "Do you want me to help pound rice?" I asked him.

"Just winnow it. Here." He picked up a round rattan tray by the side of the shed and handed it to me. "You know how, don't you?"

I nodded and took the rattan tray from him. This would be more fun than scrubbing pots, I thought. I had always liked flicking the full tray of rice grain, watching the white grain and brown husks fly up into the air, and catching the heavier grains as they rained down.

We walked into the shed, and I saw six women working in pairs inside. Each woman held a thick wooden pole and would pound a mortar filled with rice as her partner lifted her pole and waited her turn. It was dim, and dusty with the powdery rice bran, but the air was fragrant and warm. Along the back wall of the shed were stacks of bulging gunnysacks.

The cook guided me over to a corner and pointed to a mound of rice that had already been pounded, the brown husks split off from the white grain inside. I knew what I was expected to do.

Scooping up the hulled grain from that mound into my tray, I started tossing the rice up, forcing the lighter rice husks up and out of my tray. It had been a long time since I had winnowed rice, and I enjoyed doing it again. The cook watched me for a minute and nodded in approval, before turning away to leave.

Just then one of the women lifted one of the gunnysacks of rice grain and heaved it over her shoulder. As she started to pour the rice into an empty mortar, I caught a glimpse of the bag. Stenciled in green ink were the words "Rice Seed."

I stared. Rice seed—seeds of the high-yielding, long-grained rice variety that Sarun had so cherished. What these women were pounding in this shed was no ordinary unhusked rice but rice of a special variety, carefully bred and treated, so that each grain, clean and whole, would germinate in the fields back home!

I dropped my rattan tray and ran after the cook. "Wait!" I said, catching up with him. "They shouldn't be doing this."

The cook glared at me but said nothing.

I tugged at his sleeve. "It's a waste," I cried. "They're destroying rice that's meant to be planted, not eaten. Why don't they just use regular rice?"

"We've run out of it, child. With all these new recruits joining up, we've used up our supply of milled rice. And the next distribution of it won't be until after the flag-raising."

I took a deep breath. "But . . . but it's wrong!" I cried. "This is rice for farmers to plant, not for soldiers to eat!"

"Oh, be quiet!" the cook snapped. "Just take a look out there!" Roughly he pulled me to the door and gestured outside. "What do you see? Farmers or soldiers?" he demanded.

I looked. Through the narrow doorway I could see the dusty square, filled with row after precise row of soldiers standing at attention, their guns held stiffly against their shoulders.

"Well, child?" His voice was gentler now, almost sad. "You see anybody who's going to plant your precious rice seed?"

A dozen soldiers marched smartly up to the flagpole and, at some barked command, fired off their guns into the air. The gunfire resonated through the hot dusty afternoon.

I felt as if something had been torn from me, and I ached with the loss of it. Blindly I pushed past him and stumbled into the bright sunlight. No, I thought, not the rice seed, too. That's meant for us, for the women and children, for the harvest next year, for our new lives. Each rice seed, I thought, if it was carefully sown and transplanted, carefully watered and harvested, would yield fifty grains of new rice.

And now? That same kind of rice seed was being pounded and crushed, to feed these men, farmers who had, practically overnight, been turned into soldiers. It didn't make sense, I thought; none of it made any sense.

I had reached the edge of the square, and a contingent of soldiers marched past me, saluting smartly at the flagpole in front of them.

I looked down at my hand. Still cupped in my palm were some broken rice grains, the brown husks stripped off by the pounding, to expose the delicate white grain inside. None of these rice grains would sprout, or grow into tall stalks heavy with plump new rice grains. I remembered my brother's face, how flushed with hope and wonder it was, when he had shown me that first handful of rice seed as we approached the Border. With rice seed like that, Sarun had said, we could really return to our home in Cambodia and start our lives over.

A soldier marching by bumped against me and knocked the rice out of my hand. I stood back and watched his boots tread the bits of rice into the sand.

When I looked up again, that soldier had marched past. Another soldier marched by me. And another, and another. A seemingly endless series of faces flashed past.

Then I saw Sarun. His eyes straight ahead, his mouth set in a grim line, he marched right by me.

Sarun! I tried to call out to him, but nothing but a hoarse rasp came out.

In step with all the other soldiers, Sarun kept right on marching. In another instant he had turned sharply, and he was soon lost to view among the spectators on the other side of the square.

Stunned, I stood rooted to the spot. Could I have imagined it all? But no—that soldier was my brother.

Abruptly I ran along the edge of the square, trying to catch up with him. Soon I was engulfed in the crowd of onlookers on the other side. I tried to ram and elbow my way through them, but everyone was bigger and taller than I was, and I couldn't budge them.

"Sarun!" I cried. "Sarun! Wait! Sarun!"

Ahead of me, I saw a narrow break in the crowd, and began to make my way to it. Just as I was about to wriggle through, I felt someone grabbing my shoulder, pulling me back. I tried to shake the hand off, but it held on tight. Desperately, I tried to twist free, sobbing my brother's name.

Then, as if in a dream, I heard someone calling my name. The voice was low and gentle, and so full of love that I went limp. Slowly, holding my breath, not daring to hope, I turned around.

My mother opened her arms to me and drew me into them. She was big and warm and soft and she smelled like wet earth after a rainstorm. She held me and rocked me back and forth, back and forth, as if I were a baby again. And as I pressed against her, warmth against warmth and softness against softness, I could feel between us the hard round lump of the magic marble.

Chapter 13

It was the magic marble, I told them, handing the smooth ball of clay to Grandpa Kem as we all sat around the fire that evening. I had just finished telling them everything that had led up to our reunion. I was snuggled against my mother, soaking in the warmth and concern of my family. If only Chnay had agreed to join us for dinner instead of stalking off on his own, I thought with a pang of regret, he might have become part of my family.

Grandpa Kem now held the marble up and squinted at it in the firelight. "Looks like any clay marble to me," he said. "You sure it wasn't just plain old good luck that brought you back to us?" He smiled and handed the marble over to Sarun.

"It was good thinking, not good luck," Sarun countered as he took the marble. "She reasoned that she would find us back at the stone beam, and when she didn't, she and Chnay reasoned that we must have gone to Kung Silor's army camp for protection. After that, it was just a matter of time before we met up. That's all," he said, winking at me as he passed the marble to my mother without even glancing at it.

"You make it sound so simple," my mother said, taking the marble. "What about my prayers, all those nights I lay awake praying for Dara's safety?" She put her cheek on top of my head and nuzzled my hair. "Maybe it was the 'magic' marble, or maybe it was the Lord Buddha answering my prayers—what does it matter as long as you're back?"

She handed the marble over to Nea, who was sitting next to us.

"What do you think, Nea?" I asked her. "Is it a magic marble?"

Nea weighed the marble in her hand before answering. "Magic has a way of working for those who believe in it," she said slowly. "Maybe it wouldn't have been magic for someone else, but you were brave and patient, Dara, and you believed in the marble, so maybe the magic worked for you."

As she handed the marble back, she smiled at me. "Anyway, sister, I'm happy you're back with us," she said.

"Sister." Nea had called me sister. I took the marble from her and held it tightly. Was she just being affectionate, or did she mean something more? I looked at her, trying to read her smile. "I'm glad to be back, too . . . sister," I said, using the last word pointedly.

Around me, the others laughed. "Have you guessed, then?" Sarun asked.

"What?" I asked squeezing the marble. Let it be true, I begged silently. Let Nea become my sister-in-law.

"That Nea and I plan to get married soon?"

It worked! I burst into a delighted grin. No doubt about it, there was powerful magic in this marble. It felt hard and compact in my hand and even seemed a bit heavier now. It didn't matter if no one else quite believed in it. I was sure it had guided me back to the stone beam, helped me find my family, and, in some mysterious way, even linked Sarun and Nea.

Carefully I pocketed the marble, then smiled at Sarun and Nea. Their hands were linked—just like our little clay dolls', I thought. It was all happening just the way Jantu had hoped. They would get married, and our two families would all be together, living in airy, newly thatched houses by the side of the lake. Together we would sow our rice seed in the rainy season, and together harvest the fields when it turned cool. We would be surrounded by babies and bountiful harvests and peace and laughter.

"Wait till I tell Jantu!" I said gleefully. "Let's go to Khao I Dang and get her tomorrow."

"What's the rush?" Sarun asked. "There's plenty of time yet."

"But it's been over a week since I've seen Jantu," I blurted out indignantly. "I want to make sure Baby's all right!"

"I'm sure he's fine," Sarun said placatingly. "Khao I Dang is one of the most protected refugee camps around here. Besides, you can't go rushing off to see them. It's too far away to walk to, and you'd need a special pass to ride on one of the trucks or vans that go back and forth between Nong Chan and Khao I Dang."

"How do we get the special pass?" I asked.

"I'll have to ask my commanding officer," Sarun said, sticking out his chest. "It'll probably take time."

"Not too much time, I hope," Nea said quietly. "The monsoon rains are starting. If we want to prepare the seedbeds and get the rice seed sown, we'll have to leave very soon." She passed him the platter of fried banana fritters she had prepared as a special treat for this reunion dinner, and helped him to the crispiest fritter. "We should get

Jantu out and then start for home as soon as possible. Or we may miss the planting season altogether."

"The planting season?" Sarun echoed, as if he was mystified about what it was. "I can't think about planting seasons now. I've got more important things to consider."

"Like what?" I asked.

"The flag-raising, of course. It's only twelve days away," he said, his mouth full of banana. "I'm going to be marching in it, doing complex drills before the Prince."

Although he hadn't enlisted in Kung Silor's army, Sarun explained, he had volunteered to take part in the special drills, and would have to train every day.

I listened as Sarun also described, eyes glowing, how he had learned to load a gun and take aim. "You have to know how to sight the target," Sarun said, demonstrating with the rifle he had kept propped against him. He cocked his head and in deadly earnest squinted down the length of the gun. He suddenly looked so severe and belligerent that I was unnerved.

I thought of the way he had looked marching in the square that afternoon, his shoulders back, his head high, his mouth set, looking as if he had been a soldier all his life. And I suddenly realized, with a sinking feeling in my heart, that he had been enjoying himself. My brother liked being a soldier.

"What about the special pass for us to go to Khao I Dang?" Nea asked him now. "Will you ask for it tomorrow?"

Sarun frowned. "Don't rush me," he said. "I'll get around to it." He took the last fritter off the plate and stuffed it into his mouth.

There was nothing left on the platter except a few crumbs. Sarun had not even thought to pass the platter around, let alone leave anyone else a fritter or two. I reached over and took one of the crumbs. It was sweet and crunchy, and still slightly warm.

The next morning, Nea and I watched Sarun go off to his military practice. Silhouetted against the morning light, he reminded me of the times he used to go off to the paddy fields at dawn, a hoe on his shoulder. The only difference was that instead of a hoe there was now a gun.

As he disappeared into the forest, Nea sighed. It was a small, discouraged sound. "He's changed, hasn't he?" she said.

I nodded gloomily.

"I remember when I first met him," Nea continued wistfully. "He was always talking about planting a good rice crop and fishing in the lake . . ."

"I know," I said, thinking of how Sarun had told Nea how nice our village was, the day he had come back from his first mass distribution.

"He never talks about that anymore. All he seems to care about now is war and weapons, how to plant land mines, when target shooting is, how to march around in formation."

"Can't you tell him you want to go back home, to the farming, soon?"

"I've tried, Dara. There's even a caravan leaving for Siem Reap in about two weeks, and I had wanted to join it. But when I asked Sarun about it, he got angry."

"Then get angry back at him. Tell him you want—"

"I can't, Dara. I don't want to fight with him. He's going to be my husband. And besides, he said we could go on the next caravan . . ."

"Sure, or the next one, or the next one," I retorted. "At this rate, we'll be too late. If we don't make it back soon, how will we have time to plow the land and sow the rice seed?"

Nea sighed. "I don't know, Dara," she said dejectedly. "There's nothing we can do about it."

I thought for a moment. "Yes, there is," I said. "We could make the preparations for leaving now—clean and oil the oxcarts, load them up, and then pick up Jantu, all in time to join the caravan."

Nea stared at me incredulously. "All by ourselves?" she whispered. "Without telling Sarun?"

"He doesn't need to know. And he probably wouldn't be interested, anyway," I answered.

"But do you realize how heavy each sack of rice is?" Nea asked.

"We can back the carts right up to the tents where the sacks are stored," I countered quickly.

"And do you know how many sacks there are?"

"We will stack them up carefully, so the cart doesn't get lopsided."

"And what about the tools, and the nets?"

"Of course, we would have to spread the tarp over everything, and strap it down with good thick rope."

"And what about the carts? They're not even cleaned, or oiled. Our rear wheel was already creaking badly on our way here."

"We'll just have to grease the axle," I said.

"Do you know how?" Nea demanded.

"I'll learn."

Nea shook her head. "No. There's no way we could possibly do all that."

I jutted my chin at her defiantly. "We can, and we will," I said.

Frowning, Nea looked at me as if she were seeing me for the first time. "You've changed, too, Dara," she said slowly. "You didn't use to be this . . . this . . ."

"Rude?" I suggested.

Nea smiled. "Either that, or this sure of yourself," she said.

I reached in my pocket and squeezed the magic marble. "Well? Where shall we start? How about with cleaning the oxcarts?"

Nea's laugh was exasperated. "All right," she said. "We might as well give it a try."

That same morning, Nea and I dragged out my family's oxcart and swept it clean of all the broken twigs, straw, and spiderwebs that weeks of neglect had heaped on it. It was good to get on its warped planks again, to feel its rough sides and its smooth wooden wheels.

After we finished cleaning and repairing my oxcart, we did the same for Nea's. Satisfied that both were in good enough condition to make the long trip home, we turned our attention to the oxen. Like the carts, they had been neglected for some time, and looked mangy and dirty.

We led our oxen to one of the deeper mudholes and scrubbed them down there. They seemed to enjoy the water and would twist around and stare at us with their long-lashed eyes, snorting warm moist breaths on us.

"We're going home," I murmured to the smaller ox as I splashed more cool water over him. "You'll be feeling the monsoon rains on your back soon, and churning up the soft mud in the fields again. How about that?" He snorted, and Nea and I laughed.

Cleaning the oxcarts and the oxen kept us pleasantly busy for a few days, but the next step would be trickier. All the supplies we had accumulated during the mass distributions—the sacks of rice grain and rice seed, the hoe heads and rope and fishnets and tarpaulin—would have to be loaded into the oxcarts and then strapped down. This was strenuous work, usually reserved for the men.

Together we backed our oxcarts up to the tent where our sacks of rice and rice seed were stowed. We each grabbed a corner of a sack and lifted.

Half running and half stumbling with the sack of rice held between us, Nea and I headed for one of the oxcarts, probably looking very much like a crab scuttling across the sand. But we managed to reach the cart, and even to swing the sack neatly into it. Nea wiped the sweat off her forehead. "We did it," she said, sounding very surprised.

"I told you we could." I grinned, panting.

Again and again we did this, moving sack after sack from the shelter of the blue tarp and into the wagon. After a while there was a layer two deep of the precious rice-seed bags on the bottom of the oxcart.

If we planted the rice seeds with care and if the weather was good, I knew that the seeds we brought home in the cart would be enough to supply half the village next year. I felt a deep satisfaction that these seeds, at least, would not be broken and crushed to feed the soldiers here.

The next day we hauled the bags of rice grain into the carts, putting them over the rice seed. Eight sacks to a layer, three layers thick, in each of the two carts. At first Mother and Grandpa Kem were reluctant to help, fearing Sarun's anger, but then they took to giving us a hand, too.

After the bags of rice were loaded on, there was still more to be done.

We cleaned the mud and rust off the hoe heads and other tools left lying out in the open behind our shelter. Carefully we packed them in the oxcarts, on top of the rice bags. We washed and dried our clothes and scrubbed our kettle and pots. We gathered straw for the oxen for the trip home. We draped the sheet of blue plastic tarpaulin over everything, to keep things protected and dry. And finally we strapped it down with sturdy rope, double-knotting it.

By the end of it, my back was so sore that it hurt terribly even to stand straight. And Nea said her shoulders felt as if they were on fire.

But when I stood back and looked at the two oxcarts, now piled high with rice grain and rice seed, packed tight with tools and fishnets, covered with the blue tarp, and strapped with strong rope, I felt a surge of satisfaction.

Our timing had been excellent. There were three days left before Sarun's all-important flag-raising, and five before the caravan to Siem Reap would leave. All we had to do now was bring Jantu and Baby back from the hospital at Khao I Dang, wait for Sarun to perform his military rituals at the flag-raising, and then hitch our oxcarts up and drive on home!

Gratefully I held the magic marble in my hand and thanked it for having had things work out so neatly. Nothing, I thought, could hold us back now.

Chapter 14

NEA AND I took off a day to rest our sore backs, taking turns to massage each other's neck and shoulders for long stretches during the day. Then, knowing that we could not put off confronting Sarun any longer, we cornered him before he left for his military drills the next morning, his rifle propped on one shoulder.

"We've got something to show you," Nea said, gently guiding him by the elbow to the large tamarind tree where we had parked the oxcarts.

Sarun's jaw dropped in surprise when he saw that our oxcarts were already fully packed and ready to go. "Who did this?" he demanded, his voice low but angry.

"We . . . we did," Nea said evenly. "Now will you ask for the special pass to Khao I Dang?"

"Impossible," Sarun declared. "My commanding officer is very busy. The big flag-raising ceremony is tomorrow, you know. I can't bother him with details like this."

"When will you ask, then?"

"In another week or so," Sarun said carelessly. "At most two weeks."

"Two weeks!" I exclaimed. "I'm not going to wait that long. I'll ask for the passes myself. I know who General Kung Silor is. I'll go ask him."

Sarun looked alarmed. He had been impressed by the story of how I had confronted the general about the roast chicken, and I think he took my threat seriously.

"All right, I'll ask," he finally conceded.

"When?" I persisted.

"Tomorrow," he said. "After the flag-raising."

"No," I said. "Today."

His mouth set in a tight line, he went off in the direction of the officers' tent. Within a few minutes he was back, a sheet of paper in his hand.

"Here," he said, thrusting it at me. "You can take the Red Cross van from the Nong Chan gates to and from Khao I Dang tomorrow."

It was on the tip of my tongue to ask him why he had waited so long to get this special pass, if he could have gotten it so easily. But I was too relieved to be angry, and took the piece of paper from him without word.

"Can you come with us?" Nea asked him.

Sarun shook his head. "I've just been assigned sentry duty," he said. "It's my big chance. It means I can really shoot with my gun now, instead of just marching around with it."

I eyed his gun warily. "Who are you going to shoot?" I asked.

"The enemy, of course," he answered. "It's my responsibility now to protect the base camp from enemy attacks."

"What enemy attacks?" I demanded. "I haven't seen any—"

Nea put a warning hand on my arm. "Let's not argue with your brother," she murmured, with that careful sweetness edged with caution that one woman uses with another. She reached over to take the special pass away from me. "And thank you for getting this, Sarun," she said. "We'll go tomorrow, then."

"All right," Sarun said grudgingly. "But be sure you come back by nightfall. The forest trails are dangerous in the dark."

"Yes, Sarun," Nea replied meekly. Then she flashed me a mischievous smile. "Anything you say."

The next morning, Nea and I set off. At the edge of the base camp, Sarun stood guard with two other armed soldiers who were also posted there as sentries, and he saw us off. I looked back at them warily. Leaning against the palm trees, their guns pointing recklessly into the air, they looked ominous—more of a threat than a protection.

The trail through the forest back toward Nong Chan was deeply rutted. A light rain was falling on the forest trail, and the mud path was slippery and laced with deep puddles, making some sections of it almost impassable for oxcarts.

I remembered how, when we had first arrived at the Border, the oxcarts were going the other way, out of Cambodia and westward toward Thailand. Now, with the onset of the monsoon rains, long caravans of oxcarts loaded down with tools and rice seed were going the opposite way, starting on the long trek back toward Cambodia.

As we walked past each caravan, we called out greetings to the families, asking where they were headed. "Battambang," came the exuberant reply from one caravan; or "Siem Reap," from another string of oxcarts; or "Pursat, on the south side of Tonle Sap lake," the team leader of yet another caravan answered.

A creaky old cart rolled toward us, laden with sacks of rice. I saw a girl about my own age standing on the bullock cart, the reins in her hands, as her father walked beside it.

"Turn back, you're going the wrong way! Cambodia's that way!" the girl said, teasingly. "You'd better start for home before it's too late to sow your rice seed!"

"Don't worry, we'll be going home soon, too," I called out as she passed by. Still, I couldn't help but envy her as I watched her drive her laden cart homeward.

The trail improved once we emerged from the forest into the barren fields of Nong Chan. Ever since the fighting had eased off slightly in the last few days, thousands of families had moved back there and were living in their makeshift shelters again.

We threaded our way through the campsites, toward the tall bamboo watchtowers across the fields. There we presented the special pass to the relief officials, certifying that we had a sick relative at the Khao I Dang hospital, whom we were going to see. Only after that document had been thoroughly examined were we allowed to board a white van parked near one of the watchtowers.

I had never been in anything like it before, and it was exciting to be seated next to the driver, where Nea and I had a good view of the dirt road winding into Thai territory toward Khao I Dang camp. Once I got used to the dizzying speed with which the scenery flashed past the window, I watched everything with growing interest. We passed Thai village houses perched on stilts whose thatched roofs rose above the banana groves and the tamarind trees. The houses seemed so prosperous and peaceful that I felt wistful just looking at them. Stretching out on either side of the road were the rice paddies of Thailand, still brown and stubbled with the rice stalks from the past harvest. Already, however, there were patches of vibrant green where rice seedbeds had been sown and sprouted. Farmers were plowing or harrowing the rest of the fields, readying them for the transplanting of the rice seedlings from the small seedbeds into the paddy fields. It was a very familiar scene, and I longed to get home and help start the preparations for our own seedbeds. There was so much to be done before the monsoon rains began in earnest—we really had to go home soon!

I reached in my pocket and touched my magic marble lightly. Just a little more help, that's all I need, I told it. Help me find Jantu, and get us on our way homeward. That's not much to ask, is it?

It was high noon when we finally arrived at the Khao I Dang refugee camp. The camp itself was surrounded by barbed wire fencing, and at the gates were several armed guards. I felt uneasy. Were things that bad within the camp, I wondered, that barbed wire was needed to keep the people inside from escaping?

One of the guards took our special pass and motioned us to get off the van. Politely I explained why we had come, but his reply was curt and incomprehensible. Of course, I thought, he's a Thai—he doesn't speak our language. Sure enough, the guard called out to a young Cambodian nearby, and, giving him our pass, gestured at him to accompany us around the refugee camp.

Entering Khao I Dang camp was like coming into an entirely different world. Everything, absolutely everything, was in perfect order.

Moments before, I had thought the barbed wire was to keep the refugees inside. Now that I was on the other side of the fence, I realized that it was there just as much to keep people like me out. Compared to the swirling confusion of the fields at Nong Chan, this refugee camp was incredibly calm. Almost like stepping into our toy village, I thought.

The streets stretched out in neat rows ahead of me, each one clean and narrow and absolutely straight. Nea and I walked down one of them, gazing at the houses on either side. The houses all looked exactly the same—and even though they were nothing more than mud walls and a thatched roof, still they were new and neat. There were even small vegetable plots growing beside some houses, with melon vines creeping up the doorway. Whoever lived in these houses, I realized with a stab of envy, could count on staying here for a while.

Then I remembered the barbed wire and realized that these people were cooped up here like turtles in a stagnant pond, hoping only to be allowed to emigrate to some cold, distant county. And I was glad I wasn't living there after all.

Slowly I walked down the street, barely aware of Nea and the guard walking ahead. Some reddish dust from the street, stirred up by a passing breeze, settled over my bare arms. Nothing else moved. The sun beat down relentlessly, and there was not a tree in sight. The people must have retreated into the shade of their own houses, since there was nobody around.

We followed the guide through a maze of streets until we reached a huge, empty square with a water tank in the middle of it. A few children played with toy trucks made from rusty tin cans. A young woman sat breast-feeding her baby nearby. Those were the only signs of activity. The guard turned to Nea. "You know which ward your cousin's in?" he asked.

"The . . . the hospital," Nea said hesitantly.

"Yes, but which ward?" the guide repeated irritably. "Pediatric? Surgical? Malnutrition? We've got over ten different wards in the hospital area, you know." He gestured at the long thatched sheds clustered around the far end of the square. Each was the size and shape of the kitchen back at the base camp, but tacked onto each front door was a sign painted with different words and symbols. The signs made each building look very official.

"Which ward? We . . . we don't know," Nea said.

"Well, we'll try the children's ward first," he said, going into one of the sheds and motioning for us to follow him.

It was dim under the thatched roof, and I had to blink away the glare of the sun outside before I could make out what was before me.

It was the silence that first struck me. Row after row of children lay on cots of split bamboo, most of them so thin that, except for their distended stomachs, they looked like frail skeletons draped in loose skins. Too weak even to cry, these children remained completely motionless and silent. Some lay asleep in their mothers' arms; others stared blankly at the bamboo rafters.

As my eyes grew accustomed to the dim light, I saw that clipboards were hanging above each cot, often next to plastic bags dripping blood or clear fluids into thin arms. Stumbling a bit across the dirt floor, I had to stifle an urge to get away, back out into the world of sunlight and calm. But Nea gave me a gentle tug, and together we walked farther down the aisle.

"Mostly malnutrition cases," the guide said over his shoulder. "Although, of course, many of them have dysentery or malaria on top of it."

Long bony arms and legs, swollen bellies, skin flaking off a few of them, hair like straw, and always those huge, unblinking eyes.

"A lot of these children were weak already," the guide was saying to Nea, "but during the escape out of Cambodia, thousands more starved, because of Pol Pot's scorched-earth policy: his soldiers burned the villages' rice supplies just so the invading Vietnamese troops wouldn't get at them."

I thought of my own village and then of Kung Silor's soldiers, fed on rice seed, parading around the flag. How could they do this while countless children inside Cambodia starved to death?

Nea must have been thinking the same thing. In a shaky voice, she asked, "These children . . . why must the children suffer, when it's the men who are fighting?"

The guide shrugged. "What do you think this war is all about, sister?" he said.

I found it was hard to keep walking down the aisle.

Farther down was a boy who was older than the others. So thin that he seemed little more than a shadow, he might have been about my age, but he couldn't have weighed much more than Jantu's chubby baby brother. His face already looked like a skull, and his eyes were dark and sunken, though strangely glistening.

"Malaria, dysentery, and of course severe malnutrition," the guide said, glancing at the clipboard. "He doesn't have long. Three days, maybe four."

His grandmother, who was cradling him, ignored us and, slowly unbuttoning her shirt, very gently drew the boy's head toward her wrinkled breasts. He nuzzled there, and closed his eyes. Crooning, she held him close and rocked him.

Finally we were at the end of the long aisle, and I felt both sad and relieved: it was a terrible place, but at least Jantu and Baby weren't there.

The guide had gone on ahead and was waiting for us outside. "Do you have any idea where else your cousin might be?" he asked.

Nea shook her head, looking slightly dazed.

"Well, there's the surgical ward next door," he said. "You could try looking in there." He hesitated by the door, then held it open for us. "You go ahead. I'll wait for you out here."

As soon as I entered the ward, I understood why the guide chose to remain outside. It was even worse than the first shed.

Dark and gloomy, the long room was crowded with maimed people, some with their legs in plaster casts, others with bloodied gauze wrapped around their heads or chests, still others with their legs strung up to some strange metal pulleys dangling from the rafters. Many had stubs where their arms and legs should have been, the stubs wrapped in gauze stained with blood and pus. Flies swarmed around the wounds, and their buzzing merged with the soft moans of the patients. The air was filled with the smell of urine and vomit.

I took one look and turned right around. "Let's go," I whispered to Nea. "Jantu couldn't be here."

"Let's just take a quick look," Nea insisted.

Reluctantly I followed her. Slipping my hand into my pocket to hold on to the clay marble, I started down the middle aisle, peering into each face as I passed by.

Halfway across the long room, I heard someone calling my name. "Dara! At last! You're here!"

Startled, I spun around.

There stood Jantu in the middle of the shed, looking strong and healthy among all the frail, maimed patients. She waved excitedly at me.

My laugh was one of sheer relief. "Jantu!" I yelled, and ran toward her. It was so wonderful to see her that I grabbed her by the waist and hugged her hard. Nea joined us and shook Jantu's shoulders in delight, as if making sure she was real.

"And where's Baby?" I asked. "Is he all right?"

For answer, Jantu pointed to a cot farther down the aisle. Her baby brother was sitting there, playing with some rubber bands. There was a thick scar running down his ankle and along one foot, but otherwise he looked fine.

"They had to cut his foot open to take out a piece of shrapnel, but it's all healed now," Jantu said. "Come on, take a look for yourself."

We walked over to the baby, and with a joyful coo, Nea reached down and picked him up.

"Why did you take so long?" Jantu was asking me. "What happened? How's everybody? Did you find them at the stone beam?"

"Nobody was at the stone beam," I said, "but I managed to find them." And I told Jantu the rest of the story as she listened breathless and wide-eyed.

As soon as Nea left with Baby to make arrangements for us to leave, Jantu asked, "And Sarun and Nea—they're still . . . together?" "More than just 'together,'" I said, grinning. "They're getting married."

"Getting married," Jantu repeated, in an awed whisper. Her eyes were glowing. "Just like we had dreamed. So I was right! Sometimes if we dream hard enough, those dreams can shape our lives."

As if in a reverie, she dropped down to sit on the cot next to Baby's.

"Careful! Don't touch it—it hurts enough already!" a hoarse voice broke in.

Jantu looked startled and edged over to the side of the bed. "I'm sorry, Duoic," she said. "Did I hurt you?"

The gaunt figure lying on the cot smiled faintly at her. He was about thirteen or fourteen years old, with thick tousled hair and big eyes. I saw with horror that both his legs were missing, ending in bandaged stubs just above where the knees should have been. The bandages were encrusted with bloodstains and dried pus, and a few flies buzzed around them.

He saw me looking at him, and grunted. "You must be Dara, right?" he asked me.

I nodded shyly.

"Jantu has talked so much about you, but I was beginning to think you were something out of one of her stories." Despite his haggard look, a glint of mischief sparkled in his eyes, and I found myself smiling at him.

"I'm real, all right, Duoic," I said. "It just took us a while to get here."

We got to talking after that. Matter-of-factly, Duoic told me how he had lost touch with his family during their escape from Cambodia. "It was at night. I was holding on to my brother's hand when we heard some soldiers patrolling in the forest in front of us. Mother told us to hide, so we crouched in the bushes for the rest of the night. The next morning I couldn't find any of the others anymore. I panicked, and ran about shouting and looking for them." Duoic paused and frowned. "Then I guess I stepped on one of those land mines planted near the Border, and well . . . here I am."

He reached out and ran his finger across one of his bandaged stubs. There was no smile on his gaunt face now. "Jantu's lucky," he said softly. "She's got you to take her home. Me, I'll be here until . . . until . . ." He shrugged and took a deep breath. For a moment his bony chest seemed thicker, more substantial. Then he let out the air, and his chest caved in again. "Sometimes I don't know why I keep on living," he said.

I did not know what to reply, so I said nothing. Jantu, however, had taken his hand and was tugging at it gently. "That's no way to talk," she said, almost angrily. "You'll get better. How many times have I told you before: You're strong, you can make it. You've just got to keep trying!"

"Easy for you to say," Duoic mumbled. "You're healthy, and you're leaving."

"But you'll get better. You can be up and around on crutches soon."

For a moment the boy did not reply. He stared blankly at the thatched ceiling above him, and it was as if his face were hardening into an expressionless mask. Then he swallowed and whispered, "I'm thirsty." He looked at me, and his eyes were so sunken they were like tiny pinpoints of light at the end of a tunnel. "Get my water bottle for me, please," he said, pointing under his cot.

I saw a plastic bottle under his cot and reached for it. But before I could pick it up, Jantu stopped me.

"Get it yourself, Duoic!" she said sharply. "You can do it. You almost reached it yesterday."

"You get it," he begged Jantu.

"No. You can do it."

He seemed to shrink into the bed. "It's too hard," he said.

Jantu bent down so that her face was up against his. "Try!" she whispered.

The boy turned his face away from her. "I don't want to," he whispered, so softly that it sounded like the faintest breeze in the rushes. "I can't."

"You can," Jantu said, her own whisper fierce and insistent. "Go on, try it. You can do it."

"No."

"Try it!"

For a long moment the boy did not move. Then, taking such a deep breath that he seemed to grow before our very eyes, he started to hoist himself up with his arms. Inch by inch he dragged himself to the side of his bed, then slowly groped under the cot for the water bottle. Finally, with a tremendous effort, he grasped the bottle and pulled it up. Beads of sweat glistened on his forehead, but a small, triumphant smile lit his face.

"I did it," he said.

"I knew you could," Jantu said simply. She looked at him in silence for a long moment, then blurted out, "I've got to go pack now." Abruptly she got up and turned to the other cot, where she started thrusting her baby brother's few clothes into a bundle. Her movements were jerky, almost angry. "Good luck, Duoic," she said gruffly, without looking at him.

"Good luck yourself," Duoic echoed, then added softly, "And don't cry, silly. You should be happy."

I looked carefully at Jantu then, and although she kept her face carefully averted from us, I caught a glimpse of the tears glistening on her cheeks as, without a word, she strode down the aisle toward the door.

Chapter 15

IN SINGLE FILE, we walked along the narrow trail through the forest behind Nong Chan, on our way back to the base camp. The same van which had given us a lift to Khao I Dang that morning had taken us back to the Nong Chan gates. We were all tired and subdued, and for the most part we walked in silence, taking turns holding the baby.

By the time we had threaded our way across refugee campsites scattered on the plain at Nong Chan, it was early twilight, and walking into the forest was like entering a sort of green gloom. The last slats of afternoon sunlight shimmered on the puddles of the rutted path. I could barely see Jantu's footprints on the moist soil ahead of me.

"Let's stop for a rest," Nea suggested behind me. "And let me take Baby for a while, Jantu."

"You sure?" Jantu asked. "He's heavy."

For answer, Nea held out her arms. Jantu untied the checkered cloth in which the baby was secured to her, and with a small sigh of relief handed him over to Nea.

As Nea deftly tied the baby's cloth across her chest, adjusting his position so that he straddled her hip comfortably, Jantu walked over to me and put her arm around my shoulders.

"What are you thinking about?" she asked me gently. As ever, she always seemed able to sense it whenever I felt sad.

"Duoic," I answered quietly. "I wish he could have come with us."

"He wouldn't have made it," Jantu said bluntly.

"I suppose not," I said, and sighed. "It's just that . . . it's strange, I had thought that if we could go home and live together, life would be perfect. But now that we're so close to doing that, I feel sad, not happy."

"Because of Duoic?"

"And all the others like him, who won't ever be able to go home again. Why should we be able to pack up and go home when he can't?"

"Duoic doesn't mind my leaving, you know," Jantu said quietly. "He kept saying that it made him happy to think of me going back to a village to grow rice and fly kites and live out a peaceful, normal life. He wouldn't have wanted me to be trapped on the Border, like him."

"Still, it just doesn't seem fair," I said.

"Life isn't fair," Jantu said.

I thought of the Thai villages we had caught a glimpse of on the road outside Nong Chan. They had probably been there for hundreds of years without once being touched by war. No bombs were ever dropped on their paddy fields. None of their men were ever herded off to work camps. Nobody had ever been taken to the nearby forest in the depth of night, and clubbed to death. Nobody had had their legs blown off walking across a field.

"You know, if for some reason I couldn't go home with you all," Jantu mused, "I'd feel the same way Duoic did. I'd want everyone else to go on home without me. Wouldn't you?"

I frowned. The thought of leaving Jantu behind made me feel awful.

"Hey, what is all this gloomy talk?" Nea broke in, chidingly. "Come on, let's go. It's getting dark."

It was true. The twilight was turning to dusk, and soon the trail would be completely swallowed up in darkness. And we were still a good hour away from the camp.

We walked on in silence until, at a clump of wild red ginger under a big ficus tree, we came to a split in the road. Jantu stopped and looked back at us for guidance. I hadn't noticed any fork on the trail on our way out, and was not sure which path we should take now. Nea was looking uncertain, too.

"It's the one on the right, isn't it?" Nea asked me.

"I thought it was the one on the left," I said.

"Sarun said something about one of them leading to a different base camp," Nea said, "and to make sure not to take that one."

"Why not?" Jantu asked.

"Because they're our enemies," Nea said.

"But I thought the Vietnamese soldiers were the enemies," Jantu said.

"Or the Khmer Rouge," I added. "You know, Pol Pot's soldiers."

"Well, they are, too," Nea said vaguely. "But so are the people in the camps right next to ours. Sarun explained it all to me this morning, but I didn't get it too clear."

"I don't think he's too clear on it himself," I said. "He just likes the idea of having lots of enemies, now that he's been given his own gun."

"Well, he did say that if we took the wrong road, we might get shot at," Nea said nervously.

"Sounds as if we're liable to get shot at whichever road we take." Jantu snorted. "Well, do we take the right or the left?"

"The right," Nea said.

"The left," I said at the same instant.

Jantu looked at us both and laughed. "Why don't I decide?" she said. "Let's take this one." And she led us down the left fork.

The light was almost gone by now, and I could tell from Jantu's quickened steps that despite her attempt to be cheerful, she was nervous, too.

As I hurried after her, I put my hand in my shirt pocket and groped for the clay marble. It was still there, reassuringly solid. With it held tight in my fist, I felt a little better.

"I don't think this is the right way after all," I said. I looked at the clusters of ferns laced with wild clematis vines that bordered the path, and felt uneasy. "I don't remember seeing these on the way out," I said, and found that I was whispering. It was very quiet, and the forest seemed thicker and more overgrown than I had remembered. The camp was nowhere in sight.

"Let's turn back," Jantu said.

The baby whimpered, but when Nea tried to soothe him, he started to cry. The noise seemed very loud in the quiet jungle.

"Here, give him back to me," Jantu said.

"It's all right. I can—"

Just then a shot rang out, ripping apart the shroud of silence around us.

"Get down!" I shouted, and threw myself onto the ground. Nea screamed. With all my might, I grabbed her ankle and pulled her and the baby down to the ground with me.

Another shot pierced the air, even nearer this time. Nea was sobbing, her hands clutching wildly at me. I could not see Jantu anywhere.

Voices shouted at us, at first faint, then advancing closer. "Identify yourselves!" someone yelled. "Answer or we'll shoot!"

I felt a stab of shock, colder than any fear. One of the voices was Sarun's.

"Show yourself!" Sarun shouted again, just in front of us.

"It's Sarun!" Jantu shouted, running forward.

There was another shot. I heard Jantu gasp, a strangled little sound. Slowly she sank to her knees.

Even in the dusk, I could see the blood seeping through the white of her blouse. But she seemed not to notice it. There was a look of bewilderment on her face. "Wasn't that Sarun's voice?" she asked me.

The curtain of tangled vines and leaves parted, and three men burst out, each thrusting a gun at us.

"Sarun!" Nea sobbed.

Sarun stared at her, then swiveled around at the other two sentries. "Who fired that shot?" he demanded.

"I did. They refused to identify themselves, and . . ."

Sarun shook his head in disbelief. "You stupid fool!" he hissed.

"What's going on?" the other soldier asked. "You know these people?"

Before Sarun could answer, Jantu groaned. She touched her chest, then lifted her hand and examined it in the dim light. "It's dark and wet," she whispered. "What . . . what is it?" Then she swayed slightly on her knees and crumpled onto the ground.

I reached her first. Her eyes were closed, her breathing ragged. I knelt beside her and gently, my fingers trembling, started to unbutton her blouse.

"Lay her flat, on the ground," Sarun said, kneeling beside me.

As we did so, Jantu's blouse fell open, exposing her delicate collarbones. Below them, on her right side, was a wide gash from which blood was streaming.

"It looks bad," one of the soldiers grunted. "We should take her to the Khao I Dang hospital."

"What, and risk having all us of shot on the way?" the other soldier asked.

Sarun frowned. "He's right," he said after a moment's hesitation. "It'd be too dangerous now, in the dark. Besides, it's too far away. Better to take her back to the base camp, and get her onto a truck or van tomorrow morning."

I had been trying to stanch the flow of blood on Jantu's chest with a handful of leaves. I looked up at my brother and shook my head. "Jantu needs help now," I said. "We should get her back to the hospital right away."

"You heard what I said," Sarun said curtly. "It's just too dangerous now. There'll be plenty of vehicles heading out after the flag-raising tomorrow. We'll get her a ride to the hospital on one of them."

"That will be . . . " Too late, I had wanted to say. But Sarun had already turned his back to me and was talking to the other soldiers. I felt a wave of panic building up in me. Then Jantu stirred, and though her breathing was ragged, she managed a faint smile.

"That'd be fine," she said, finishing up my sentence for me. "Maybe by the morning I'll be all right, and won't even need to go back to the hospital. Right, Dara?"

Blood was seeping through the layer of leaves and out between my fingers, where I had clumsily tried to hold them against her wound. "Yes, Jantu," I said softly. "You'll be fine by morning." And I was glad that she closed her eyes then, because otherwise she would have been able to tell that I was lying to her.

Chapter 16

WHEN WE GOT JANTU BACK to the base camp, my mother tended
to her as best she could. By the flickering light of a borrowed kerosene
lamp, Mother gently peeled away the wad of leaves I had clamped
over the wound, and rinsed the blood away. Exposed on Jantu's chest
now was a jagged gash between her right nipple and belly button,
where the bullet had ripped into her. The bullet must have still been
lodged somewhere inside her, since her back was smooth and un-
marked. But when Mother tried to press down gently to see where it
was, Jantu moaned so pitiably that she didn't dare probe any further.
Instead, she took a clean sarong, ripped it into strips, and bound
Jantu's chest with it.

Despite the pain that Jantu obviously felt while her wound was
being dressed, she fell into a fitful sleep almost immediately afterward.

I brought over my sleeping mat and curled up on it, and fell asleep
lying next to Jantu.

I woke up every time Jantu moaned, and would watch helplessly as
she tossed her head fretfully from side to side. Sometimes I would
stroke her arm, as if my running my hand up and down her smooth
dry skin, I could take away some of her pain.

Several times during the night, I took out the clay marble and
prayed that it could restore Jantu's strength and make her well again.

"Just one more time," I begged it silently, holding it tight in my
fist. "Make Jantu well, and I will never ask for anything again."

Toward morning, when I tried to calm her down by putting my
hand on her cheek, I noticed how hot she was. In alarm, I called my
mother and Nea over, but there was little they could do other than
put cool, damp rags on her forehead.

Jantu's fever abated as dawn broke, but her face still looked
flushed. As Nea bent over to change the damp rag on her forehead,
Jantu woke up and blinked sleepily. Her eyes wandered over the
thatched palmetto roof of the shelter, then rested on me. She

brightened, and for a moment a shadow of her old cocksure grin flashed across her face.

"Dara! You're really here," she murmured. "So I didn't dream it all." She tried to get up, and her smile changed abruptly to a grimace of pain. Bewildered, she glanced down at her chest and saw the sarong strips wound tightly around it. Splotches of blood had seeped through the cloth and stained it a rusty brown. She started to take a deep breath, then stopped when she realized how much even that pained her. Dumbly she looked at me in appeal.

"You're hurt, Jantu," I told her. "Don't try to get up."

"What happened? Tell me," she demanded in a hoarse whisper.

And so, as simply as I could, I told her how Sarun and two other sentries had mistaken us for enemies in the dark, and fired at us, accidentally wounding her. But she was going to get well, I told her quickly. As soon as the flag-raising was over that morning, we would get her on one of the many vehicles that had made their way to the base camp, and get her back to the hospital. She would get proper medical treatment there, I assured her. She would recover quickly, and then we would all go home on our oxcarts, just as we had planned.

As I talked, I watched her anxiously, and it was as if a mask had descended on her face, making it blank and hard. With a stab of dread, I realized that I had seen the same mask settle on Duoic's face the day before, when he had refused to reach for the water bottle. It was the look of someone who wasn't going to try anymore.

"You will get better, Jantu," I said desperately.

For answer, Jantu only closed her eyes. There were dark green shadows under them, and her cheekbones seemed to jut out more sharply. I watched her bandaged chest rise and fall, and it seemed that her breathing had become even more shallow and ragged.

Sarun came into the shelter, ducking his head under the thatched eaves. "How is she?" he asked, in a cheerful voice that seemed to fill up the whole room.

Nea, who was sitting nearby, shushed him and motioned him to go back out, following him out as she did so. Through the thin thatched walls, I heard their whispered conversation.

Nea wanted to try to find a vehicle to get Jantu to the hospital now, but Sarun insisted that there was nothing he could do, that nobody would be leaving until after the flag-raising, which would be over in a few more hours anyway.

"I've got to go march in it," he said impatiently. "You're coming to watch, aren't you? You promised you would." It wasn't a question but a demand.

Nea must have recognized the peremptory tone in Sarun's voice, for after a moment's hesitation she agreed.

"How about the others?" Sarun was demanding now. "Mother and Dara and Grandpa Kem? Weren't they all supposed to come, too?"

I leaned out the opening of the shelter, and said, "I'm not going. I'm staying with Jantu."

Jantu's eyes flickered open at the sound of her own name, and she said weakly, "No, you go along. I'll be fine."

But I could be as stubborn as my brother, and I insisted that I wasn't going anywhere. In any case, Sarun didn't seem to care much one way or the other whether I would watch him parade around the square. I guess it was really just the grownups, especially Nea, that he wanted to impress.

And so, to humor Sarun, it was agreed that Nea and my mother would go along to the flag-raising, leaving Grandpa Kem behind to do some chores, and to keep us company.

"We'll be back as soon as the flag-raising ceremony is over," Nea told Jantu gently, brushing away a wisp of hair from her cousin's eyes.

"Don't worry, I'll be fine," Jantu said. "But before you go, could you move me into the hammock outside?" she asked Sarun. "I want to be under the open sky. I can't seem to breathe properly in here."

And so Sarun lifted her up in his arms and carefully laid her in the hammock. I saw how much it pained her to be moved, even though she tried not to show it.

Once she was settled into the hammock, however, she looked happier and more relaxed.

Nea and Sarun and Mother left the two of us with the baby, as Grandpa Kem wandered off to gather some straw for the oxen. Jantu waved goodbye to them weakly from her hammock.

It was quiet after they left. The families around us had also gone to watch the ceremony, and we were the only ones around. I leaned back against the tree by Jantu's hammock. Her baby brother was sitting on the ground, scratching circles in the sand with a twig.

"I'll be glad when this flag-raising is over," I said, tugging at the hammock rope gently to get it rocking. "Then Sarun will finally agree to leave, and we can all head home."

Dreamily Jantu watched the canopy of leaves swing by overhead. "Do you really think so, Dara?"

"Of course," I said with forced cheerfulness. "Our carts are packed. The caravan is due to leave in three days. All we have to do is to make you a comfortable nest on top of your cart, and then we'll start driving east."

"I was talking about Sarun," Jantu said. "Do you really think he'll be ready to leave with this caravan?"

"I don't see why not," I said.

"Don't you, Dara? Listen." She gestured in the direction our families had just gone, toward the parade ground.

From the loudspeakers around the square came the sound of strident marching songs. As we listened, the music was replaced by the sound of a voice. It was high-pitched, charged with a fervor clearly designed to be infectious. Long, glib phrases came snaking out of the forest.

"As part of the great revolutionary cause," the voice blared, over the crackling static of the loudspeaker system, "we must wage a struggle against the puppets and lackeys of our enemies. We must strive to be anti-colonialist, anti-Vietnamese, anti-imperialist . . ." The words trailed like paper streamers through the air, fluttering for a moment before being dispersed by the breeze.

"Who was that?" I asked.

"Does it matter?" Jantu said. "They all say the same thing. They seem to think it's a game." Her voice was low and fierce, and she spoke quickly, as if the words had been pent up in her for a long time. "They take sides, they switch sides, they play against each other. Who wins, who loses, whose turn it is to kick next—it's like an elaborate soccer game. Except that they don't use soccer balls. They use us."

Jantu paused, and in the quiet we could hear the voice over the loudspeakers again. "We must keep fighting for the future of Cambodia. We must plant more land mines, arm ourselves with more weapons, fire more bullets—until we kill every last one of the Enemy Number One!" again there was loud applause.

Jantu smiled. "Look at me," she said gently. "Do I look like your Enemy Number One? And my friend Duoic—whose enemy was he? Oh, Dara, at the hospital I saw so many people brought in, day after day, bleeding and maimed. Most of them weren't even soldiers. Why do they keep shooting at us, Dara? Why?"

I did not know the answer, so I kept silent.

"And the fighting's not going to stop," Jantu went on, her voice low and vehement. "Look what's happening around us. There are far more guns than farm tools being distributed, far more bullets than rice seed. Yet they talk about the future of Cambodia, about rebuilding the country. Does that make any sense to you, Dara?"

Again, I did not know what to say. For a long moment there was only silence. A fly buzzed around Jantu's bandages, alighting on a bloodstain there. I waved it away. "Don't think about such things, Jantu. Just rest up, and everything will be fine."

"Everything will not be fine," Jantu said. "Face it, Dara, things are not going well. I'm not sure that we'll ever make it home."

"Of course we will," I said soothingly. "As soon as you are well enough to travel, we'll join a caravan and head for home."

Jantu shook her head. "Not even then," she said. "Not even if I get well."

"Why not?"

"Because Sarun won't go."

"Yes he will. We'll make him go," I said.

With great effort, Jantu propped herself up on her elbow on the hammock and looked me right in the eye. "Who will make him?" she asked.

"We will."

Jantu shook her head at me sadly. "Not 'we' Dara," she said. "You'll have to do it. Alone."

"Why me?"

"Because," she said softly, "I don't think I'll be around to help you."

The rock. That sudden punch of pain, like a rock slamming into my stomach. I recognized that pain from the day of the shelling near the food truck, when Jantu had said, "Lost: we're lost." And now I felt it again, that rock-hard pain.

"No," I whispered. "In just a couple of hours we'll take you to the hospital. You'll get better there."

"Face it, Dara. If you want to go home, you've got to make Sarun leave. I've done all I can. I can't do any more." Her breathing was so shallow that her chest was barely moving. I noticed that fresh blood was seeping through her bandages.

"No," I said. "No."

"Listen to me, Dara. I can't help you anymore. You've got to do the rest."

"No." No, no, please no—in the sudden silence of my fear, I remembered my father's voice the night he was dragged away to be killed in the forest. I had lain there, I had heard the dread and the fear in his voice—and I had felt the fear lodge in my own heart. Yet he had begged so softly. Was it because he hadn't wanted to wake me up? No, no, no, he had murmured, and as I lay there in the dark, all I could do was to echo in my heart "no." And then there was only the silence.

I felt Jantu's hand on my arm, warm and firm. "Yes, Dara," she was saying. "I know you can do it." She looked at me, her eyes steady and calm.

I pushed the fear and the dread and the voices away, and I tried instead to listen to Jantu's voice, warm and gentle. "Remember when you didn't want to go alone to look for our families, Dara?" she said. "After Baby was wounded? Remember how scared you were then? But you did it, Dara. You went off and found our old campsite, and then you found our families again. You did it, Dara. And you can do it again now."

"But that wasn't me," I said. "It was the magic marble you gave me."

"Magic marble?" A tired smile flickered across Jantu's face. "You really believed in that? In that magic marble?"

"It worked," I said.

"It worked," Jantu said gently, "because you believed it would. That's all."

"Then just make me another one. A bigger one, with stronger magic. I'll believe in that one, too." Desperately I scooped a lump of damp clay from a nearby puddle and tried to give it to Jantu. She wouldn't take it, but I pressed it into her left hand. "Please," I begged her.

Jantu only looked at the lump of clay on her palm, moist and shapeless. Slowly she closed her hand around it, but she made no move to mold it. Except for the sound of her shallow breathing, it was quiet.

I noticed then that she seemed to be having more trouble breathing. Each breath of air she sucked in seemed to cause her pain. Then, with a great effort, she spoke again. "You've got to believe in yourself, Dara. Not me. Not magic marbles. There's no magic in that marble I gave you, or in this lump of clay in my hand. The magic is only in the making of the marble. You've got to do it on your own."

"Do what?" I asked. "Make my own marble?"

Jantu smiled faintly. "Yes," she said. "Make your own magic marble."

"But, Jantu, I can't. I don't know how. I don't have magic in my fingers the way you do. Please, Jantu, make me one more magic marble. Just one more."

"No," Jantu whispered, and closed her eyes. "You've got to do it yourself." For a long moment there was no sound except the rustling of the leaves overhead.

Jantu looked as if she was about to drift off to sleep, but with an effort she opened her eyes again. "Give me Baby," she told me. "I want to hold him."

I reached down and picked up her baby brother and gently placed him against her left side, where he wouldn't disturb her wound. Tucked against Jantu in the hammock, he gurgled happily. Jantu nuzzled her cheek against his hair and sighed. "Now rock us, Dara," she said quietly. "We're going to sleep."

And so I started to push the cloth hammock, push and swing, to and fro, back and forth. The rhythm of it was soothing.

"Sing to us, Dara," Jantu said softly. "Rock us and sing us to sleep."

I hesitated. "What shall I sing?" I asked.

"Sing about home," Jantu said dreamily. "Home, where we can splash in the paddy fields, and feel the raindrops on our skin, and hear the crickets crying at night . . ." Her voice faded, and she breathed a deep sigh. "Sing me to sleep," she whispered, her voice like dry wind sweeping over the wild pampas grass.

Gently I pushed the hammock to and fro. And then, softly, I sang the lullaby she had taught me, that day when we first played with our village by the ancient stone beam, with the rain drumming on the palm fronds above us, the same lullaby her mother had sung to her:

> "When the rain is falling,
>   When the rice is growing,
>   When the day is done,
>   Then my little one, my lovely one,
>   Will come home to sleep—and dream."

I watched Baby's eyes flutter as he fought sleep for a few minutes, before they closed, heavy-lidded. His breathing became deep and regular.

Jantu, too, watched over him until he was asleep. Yet even after that, she did not close her own eyes. Glowing with a dull sheen, they gazed through me, at something far away. She had a strangely remote smile on her face.

I kept rocking the hammock, and singing, and eventually Jantu closed her eyes, too, and it seemed as if she was closing herself off from me, and my song, and the world around us. And it was then that the fear and the dread welled up in me again. I wanted to shake her, to wake her up so she would come back to me.

But I only kept singing. Even after Jantu's long, slim fingers went limp, I kept on singing. I rocked and I sang, and I sang and I rocked, not daring to stop, for fear of waking the baby, but more than that, deeper than that, for fear of finding out that my friend Jantu would never wake up again.

Chapter 17

I WAS STILL ROCKING the hammock when the others came back. Sarun was walking slightly ahead of Nea and Mother and seemed to be in a state of high excitement. He was saying loudly over his shoulder to them, "I don't care what the rest of you think! I'm going to enlist! I've made up my mind. It is the only patriotic thing to do."

"Not so loud," I warned Sarun. "You'll wake them up." Jantu and her baby brother lay quietly curled together in the hammock. It seemed terribly important that they not be disturbed yet. I tugged at the hammock rope, careful to keep it swinging with the same gentle rhythm.

Sarun ignored me. "Did you see the way hundreds of men enlisted after the speech?" he asked the others, his voice as strident as before.

"Be quiet," I begged him. "You'll wake them up!"

Sarun glanced at the hammock. "So let them wake up!" he said loudly. "Let them see what a real soldier looks like!" He grabbed the rope from me and gave it a wild tug.

"No!" I cried, trying to snatch the rope back from him.

"Time to wake up!" Sarun announced.

I pulled the rope back from him, desperately trying to steady the hammock.

But it was too late.

The baby woke up, wailing.

I let go of the rope and watched it trail across the dust, following the hammock. Wake up, Jantu, I begged silently, please wake up.

The hammock slowed down, little by little, until it stopped swinging and reached a complete stop.

The baby kept wailing, but Jantu—Jantu did not wake up.

As if in a dream, I watched Nea pick up the baby and comfort him. Then she bent over the hammock and reached out to touch Jantu's cheek. I watched as a slow understanding dawned on Nea's face. She uttered a small cry. I watched as Mother and Grandpa Kem rushed to the hammock and looked inside. I felt numb, and though I was standing right there, I felt that I was very far away, as if I were watching it all from a great distance.

Nea was crying now, her head buried in the baby's neck as he sobbed, too. Sarun patted her back awkwardly, trying to comfort her.

"She's gone," Nea was sobbing. "She's gone, and I want to go, too. I want to go home. I want to go home." Like a kite string suddenly snapped in two and left to flail in the wind before dropping down, Nea went limp and helpless. Mother and Grandpa Kem stood quietly nearby, too stunned to do anything.

"Nea's right," I said. "It's time to go home."

"We can't leave right now," Sarun said.

"Why not?" I asked.

"Because I've decided to enlist as a regular in the army, that's why. I belong here now. I'm not going to leave."

I felt a chill go through me. "Enlist?" I said softly. "You don't mean it."

Sarun looked at me. "I do," he said.

"Why?"

"You wouldn't understand," he said. "It has to do with being a soldier. With defending the revolutionary cause. It has to do with a man's courage."

It scared me, how much I hated my brother then. I took a deep breath. "Courage?" I echoed. "You talk of courage? What courage does it take to shoot a girl walking home in the dark? What courage did it take to kill Jantu?" My voice broke, and I wanted to crumple up and cry, too, the way Nea was doing. But Jantu had told me to be strong. Jantu had said I had to believe in myself.

I looked into the hammock at her and saw the lump of clay still cupped in her hand. You have to do it yourself, she had said; you have to make your own magic marble. I bent over and picked up the clay. It was damp and cool and heavy. Hesitantly I started to roll it between my hands. And as I rolled it, I began to feel calmer.

"What about going home?" I said, my voice controlled now. "What about planting rice and raising a family? What about trying to live in peace, when there is a war going on? Doesn't that take courage, too?"

Sarun avoided my eyes. "You're just a child, Dara," he said. "You wouldn't understand war."

"Don't tell me I don't understand war," I said fiercely. My hands seemed to have a life of their own, kneading and rolling, shaping that cool ball of clay. "I understand that Jantu will never wake up in that hammock again. I understand that Father will never come home to us again. I understand that war kills people who aren't even fighting in it." My eyes stung, and when I blinked, I could feel the threads of cool tears streaking my cheeks. But my hands were still shaping my marble, smoothing it, and I did not bother to wipe my tears away. "What I don't understand, Sarun, is why you want to fight. You said you'd take us home. The carts are all packed. The caravan is waiting. Why can't we go, Sarun? Why can't you stop fighting, and take us home?"

For a moment my brother looked up at me, and his eyes were bewildered and lost, too. Then he shook his head. "Because I am going to enlist," he said. "And as a soldier I have to stay on to fight this war. As for going home to plant rice—any woman or child can do that."

The ball of clay grew smoother and rounder. "You're right, Sarun," I said quietly. "Anyone can do that. So that's what I am going to do. I am going home now, to plant that next crop of rice."

"You?" Sarun snorted. "You and who else?"

"Just me," I answered. "I'll take a sack of our rice seed, and our oxcart, and join the caravan going to Siem Reap, and once I'm back home, I will find people to help plant the seeds with me. I'll fix up our house, repair the floorboards and the thatching on the roof. I'll tend the rice fields, and feel the raindrops on my skin, and listen to the cry of crickets at night. I've had enough of this horrible place, Sarun. I'm leaving." My voice and my hands were trembling, but the ball of clay was very smooth now.

For a long moment no one said anything. Then my mother stepped forward and stood beside me. "I'm coming with you, Dara," she said gently. "I don't think I can bear to be here much longer either. And without Jantu, there is no reason to delay our trip anymore."

Sarun's mouth dropped. "You . . . you can't do that," he said.

Mother looked at him. "Why not?" she asked.

Sarun turned to Nea. "Talk some sense into them, will you?" he demanded. "They can't take the cart and leave, just like that. It's ridiculous."

Nea shifted the baby over to her other hip. In the twilight, her tears still shone wet on her cheeks. "It's not ridiculous," she said. "It's the only sensible thing to do. And I'm going with them. And bringing Baby with me, too."

She looked at Grandpa Kem. "Are you coming?" she asked.

Grandpa Kem nodded. Then, without a word, he walked over to his oxcart. "It's all ready to go," he said. "And I'm ready to go with it."

We all watched Sarun. He looked hard at each of us, then at the oxcarts. He turned to me, his eyes angry and dazed. "I thought I was the head of the family," he said shakily. "You can't make decisions like that."

"You are still the head of our family," I said quietly. The marble was big and heavy in my hand. I kept molding it, my movements deft and sure now. "We need you to come home with us, brother. Please come."

Sarun stared at me, almost as if I were a stranger to him. For a moment I thought he was going to turn away, but he was only laying down his gun. With his bare hands outstretched, he walked slowly toward Nea.

"All right," he told her quietly. "The monsoon rains are coming soon. It's time to go home and plow the fields."

Wordlessly, Nea took his hands in hers.

It was then that I was aware of my own hands, still clenched tightly together. I relaxed, and opened up my hands. In the dappled play of light and shadow from the web of sunlit leaves above, it was hard to make out at first what I was holding. Only gradually could I see that cupped in my palm was a perfectly smooth, perfectly round marble.

I looked away at Jantu's cupped hand, now empty and lying motionless in the hammock. I did it, Jantu, I told her silently. I made my own magic marble.

Chapter 18

I<small>T WAS STILL DARK</small> when I woke up. Turning toward the opening of the thatched shelter, I looked out at the night sky. A full moon gleamed through a web of branches, and a bright morning star shone near it. The only hint of dawn was a faint glow to the east, so dim it was just a pale shade of gold-gray.

Why had I woken up so early? There had been no sudden noise, no clap of thunder, no gunfire or sound of shelling. Except for the whine of a mosquito, it was absolutely quiet. What had woken me up? And why did the morning feel so special?

Then I remembered: today was the day we were to leave.

Even now I could hardly believe it. Was it really happening, what I had dreamed of for so long? Yes, I reassured myself, we were going home, all of us, my family and Jantu's.

Jantu. That familiar heaviness, like an ache deep inside, settled on me again. The day after she died, we had taken her to the small clearing deep in the forest where two low brick walls had been built for cremations. I had gathered some wildflowers from the woods that morning and placed a bouquet of wild cleome and morning glories over her. The flowers had already wilted, and I did not stay to see them crinkle up in the flames.

Thinking about Jantu now, I wished I had given her something more, something that I had woven or shaped, something I had made, like all the things she had made and given me.

I sat up and took my two magic marbles out of my shirt pocket. The larger one was Jantu's, and the smaller one mine. I could have given her these two marbles, I thought. But what use would she have had for them? I looked at the marbles now, and the ache inside me grew sharper. I miss you, I told Jantu; I wish you were coming with us.

Nearby, the others were beginning to stir. My mother had already rolled up her sleeping mat and slipped outside. Through the cracks in the loose thatching, I could see her gathering an armful of straw to feed the oxen. Nea was up, too, stoking the embers of the cooking fire to warm up some cold rice for a quick breakfast.

"Dara," Nea was calling. "Come have some rice now. We'll be leaving right after we eat."

I took a deep breath and slipped the two marbles back into my pocket. Then I went outside.

There was a general sense of excitement in the air. My brother had begun to hitch up the carts, and Grandpa Kem was helping him. Mother was folding the last of the sarongs she had washed and hung out the night before. Even Baby was busy, crawling around and exploring the ground under the oxcarts.

I saw a lone figure slip out of the shadows of the nearby trees and hurry toward us. Even before I could see his face, I knew it was Chnay. I was surprised, but glad, too. Ever since I had found my own family, he had avoided me, even though I had invited him to eat with us several times. But he had always refused, claiming that he felt more comfortable eating by himself. I waved to him now, and waited for him to come up to me.

"I . . . I brought you something," he said awkwardly. He held out a wooden cowbell, polished to such a high sheen that it gleamed in the morning light.

"Where did you get it?" I asked.

Chnay smiled. "I made it," he said with pride.

I thought of the way he used to break Jantu's toys, smashing them to the ground and laughing. It was hard to think of him making anything.

He must have seen the surprise on my face, because he smiled. "The first two bells I carved didn't turn out very well. This is my third try."

"Thanks, Chnay," I said.

"Actually," Chnay said, awkwardly, "I made it for Jantu. At least, I was thinking about her when I made it." He walked over to our pair of oxen and started to tie the bell around the bigger one's neck. I went over to the ox and stood on its other side. As he busied himself with tying the bell, Chnay continued, "I thought of the way she used to make things out of sticks and scraps and mud and, well . . . I felt bad that I had broken so many of them."

"Jantu would have liked your bell very much," I said shyly, stroking the muzzle of the ox. It tossed its head, swinging its new bell. It was a lovely sound, the low wooden knock-knock of it. Chnay and I smiled at each other.

"Why don't you come back with us?" I said. "You'll like our village."

He kept smiling, but his eyes turned sad. "I wouldn't belong there," he said.

"You think you belong here?"

Chnay shrugged. "Here, at least I won't feel so out of place. I mean, there are a lot of loners like me, boys without any family." Chnay paused. "I've gotten to know some of them already. And guess what? I've made friends with that monkey, too." He flashed me a smile, and then he was gone, running off without a backward glance, his bare feet kicking up sprays of water as he splashed through the puddles between the trees.

By midmorning everything was ready. Our oxen were hitched to the two oxcarts, each bulging with its pile of rice bags and tools, and the blue tarp stretched on top. Nearby, in a crooked line, the other oxcarts in the caravan were waiting, ready to start.

"Climb up," Sarun shouted over to me.

I walked over to our oxcart and climbed onto the wooden plank in front. There I took a last look around.

On the parade ground, soldiers were still doing their drills, and beyond them, I could hear the rhythmic pounding of rice seed in the little shed. Behind the grove of jacaranda trees, over the thatched roof of the kitchen, I could see the blue-and-white Khmer Serei flag, fluttering in the morning breeze.

Nea climbed up, too, and sat next to me, hugging the baby to her.

In the cart in front of us sat Grandpa Kem and my mother, looking radiant. Sarun was going to walk alongside their cart, leading the oxen.

As if sensing the excitement, the animals were pawing at the ground and tossing their heads up and down. People ran about, calling out farewells, gathering a few stray belongings, making last-minute checks of the harnesses or the ropes, before climbing onto their oxcarts.

Then the team leader stood straight up in the first cart and flicked his whip high in the air, "Hooo!" he shouted, and his oxen lumbered forward, pulling the cart along with them.

Mother's cart was the next. Sarun turned around, his eyes shining. "Ready?" he called and, without waiting for our answer, tugged the oxen forward.

It was our turn now.

"You take the reins," Nea said excitedly. "I've got Baby," I gripped the reins in my hand so tightly that my fingers felt numb.

"Come on," Nea urged me.

I nodded, then tugged at the reins. Creaking loudly, the wheels started rolling. Behind me, I could hear driver after driver shouting at his oxen, as each started up his cart in turn.

Farther ahead, Sarun was guiding his oxen on a path into the forest, away from the camp's clearing. The path that wound through the trees was narrow and uneven, edged with long puddles where previous ruts had filled with rainwater.

Following Sarun's oxcart, I pulled at my reins, veering the oxen onto the narrow path. There was a big bump as a cartwheel dipped into a rut.

As we lurched forward, the bigger of the two clay marbles inside my pocket flew out into the air and rolled into a puddle.

"Jantu's marble!" I cried. I tried to rein in the oxen, but they just plodded along, intent on following the cart ahead. Frantically I stood up, prepared to jump off the cart after the marble.

"What're you doing ?" Nea asked, alarmed.

"Jantu's marble! It slipped out and—"

"We can't stop for it. You'll hold up the whole caravan!"

"But she made it! It's all I have of her." I was on the verge of tears. "It's her magic marble."

Nea reached out and put her hand on my shoulder. "The magic was never in the marble, sister," she said. "It was in Jantu. And now it's in you."

For a long moment I stared at the puddle into which Jantu's marble had disappeared. The last ripple had faded, and there was not a trace of the clay marble left. Slowly I took the other marble out of my pocket, the one I had made myself, and held it. Round and smooth and hard, it lay there in my palm.

I looked at it, and for the first time I saw it for what it was: just a lump of clay. There was no magic in it, I realized. Not in the one Jantu made, nor in the one I made. And then I finally understood what Jantu had meant when she had said the magic is in the making of the marble.

I held my marble a moment longer. Then I stood up in the oxcart and, taking a deep breath, flung the marble away.

It sailed through the air, rolled to the side of the road, and slipped into the same strip of puddle as Jantu's marble. There was a tiny splash, a few ripples, and then it, too, was gone.

I sat back down and snapped the reins. The oxen lumbered forward, and the cartwheels turned a little faster. Our cart rolled ahead, smooth and fast.

Nearby a skylark sang, perched on a sandalwood tree. The morning air was fresh and cool, and the sky a cloudless blue. Through the trees in the forest, I could see patches of vibrant green rice seedlings, rippling in the breeze.

And all around me was the sound of cowbells, the brass ones tinkling, the bamboo ones tapping like tiny drums, the shiny bronze ones jangling; but the most beautiful sound of them all was the low knocking of the wooden bell dangling from our own ox.

I tossed my head back and laughed out loud, in sheer joy. I'm going home, I thought, and I don't need magic marbles anymore. After all, the magic isn't in the marble. It's in me!

Afterword

THAT WAS over ten years ago.

We have been lucky, my family and I. We were among those to return from the Border safely and settle back into our village in Siem Reap. We planted our first crop with the precious rice seed we were given at Nong Chan, and our harvest that year was a good one.

Sarun and Nea have three children now, two boys and a girl. They live just across the fields from us. Mother lives with them, but comes to visit me almost every other day.

The years have been difficult, but we have survived. Cambodia is still a country at war, and there continues to be fighting in scattered areas, especially around the Border, but so far it has not touched us directly. There are still heavily armed soldiers there, the Khmer Rouge and Khmer Serei and the Khmer People's National Liberation Front, still merging and splitting into uneasy alliances with one another and against the Vietnamese-backed Heng Samrin government. Sometimes over the radio I hear reports of a peace plan being negotiated in some foreign city, but nothing ever seems to come of it. Meanwhile, the war continues, and the fighting continues. It makes no more sense to me now than when I was a little girl at the Border.

I don't think about what happened on the Border very much anymore. But sometimes, on an afternoon like this, when the monsoon wind is stirring the palm fronds, when the skies are alive with swallows and homemade kites, diving and dipping above the green paddy fields, when the young rice stalks ripple in sweeping waves, then I sit on the steps of our little house, and the images of the Border sweep like swallows through my mind.

I see many sad things—that gaunt hollow-eyed boy with no legs, reaching for his water bottle; those silent women, pounding the rice seed into bits of broken grain; the lost little girl with the broken doll, crying for her mother.

But of Jantu I have only happy images. I see her the way she was at the well the first day, bossy, cheerful, loud. I see her running after the food truck, hitching Baby up her hip as she ran. I see her singing her lullaby in the twilight after the rain, her eyes shining, to our little clay dolls.

I make pretty good clay dolls myself now. I shape farmers and plump babies, buffaloes and ducks, and give them to my daughter to play with. That's right, I have a daughter now, a toddler with chubby fingers and sparkling eyes. My husband dotes on her and is always urging me to make her more clay toys.

There is one thing I haven't made for her, and that is a clay marble. I know I can make them, the way Jantu taught me, smooth and round and hard. But I am not going to make any yet. When the time comes, I want to teach her how to make a magic marble, for herself.

Related Readings

**Miriam
Greenblatt**

from
Cambodia

*The people of Cambodia won independence from
France in the early 1950s. In the years that followed,
opposing groups inside and outside the country gained
control of the government. As this recent history of
the country shows, the opposing groups often used
violence against the people. Hundreds of thousands of
Cambodians made the choice Dara and her family in*
The Clay Marble *made—to escape the fighting by
crossing the border into neighboring countries.*

From Independence Through Revolution

Independence did not bring Cambodia political stability. Over the
next forty years the country had four different governments. First
came one-man rule by Norodom Sihanouk, from 1953 to 1970. Then
came a republic, from 1970 to 1975. The period from 1975 to 1979
witnessed a Communist revolution led by the Khmer Rouge.[1] And in
1979 Cambodia once again came under Vietnamese control.

Sihanouk in Power

To everyone's surprise Sihanouk remained king for only two years. In
1955 he gave up the throne in favor of his father, Norodom
Suramarit. Sihanouk, however, did not give up political power. Quite
the contrary. He established a national political movement called
Sangkum Reastr Niyum, "People's Socialist Community," and declared
himself its "nonpolitical" leader. It was a shrewd move. Sihanouk was
immensely popular as the "father of Cambodian independence."

---

1. **Khmer Rouge** a radical communist group in Cambodia

Moreover, most Khmers[2] considered him semidivine[3] and therefore entitled to their vote. Accordingly, when elections for the Assembly were held in September 1955, the Sangkum won every seat. The existing political parties soon disappeared, and Sihanouk ran the country as both prime minister and foreign minister. When his father died in 1960, Sihanouk also received the title of chief of state.

Sihanouk tried to make life better in many ways for the Khmers. Elementary schools and hospitals were built in rural areas, and a medical school and a nursing school were established in Phnom Penh. The capital also boasted several water purification plants. The government nationalized, or took control of, such industries as banking, foreign trade, and insurance, and replaced Chinese and Vietnamese workers with Khmers. Unfortunately, one result of nationalization was that foreign businesses stopped investing in Cambodia. In addition, many of the nationalized businesses were poorly run. So the only people who really benefited were Sihanouk's friends, who received special favors from the government-owned enterprises.

Nevertheless, it was clear that Sihanouk truly cared about his people. He was also a born showman. As one historian pointed out: "He toured the kingdom tirelessly, delivering three- and four-hour speeches at top speed and sometimes, when he was angry, at the top of his voice. In these talks, delivered in slangy, colloquial Khmer, the prince made fun of his opponents and foreigners, while praising his 'children,' Angkor, and the achievements of the Sangkum." He starred in and directed several feature films. He edited various publications, including a French-language magazine and a Khmer-language comic monthly. And he wrote hundreds of letters to foreign newspapers criticizing every article that suggested Cambodia was anything short of perfect.

Troubles Arise

Sihanouk remained immensely popular until the 1960s. Then he began running into trouble.

Ever since the end of Word War II a cold war had been raging between the United States and its allies on one side and the Soviet Union and its allies on the other side. Both sides wanted Cambodia's

---

2. **Khmers** people who are native to Cambodia
3. **semidivine** half mortal and half divine

support. Sihanouk, however, felt that "When the elephants fight, the grass is trampled." To him, Cambodia's safest course was to remain neutral.

Problems arose because of Vietnam. In 1954, one year after Cambodia became independent, France was forced to grant Vietnam its independence as well. However, the country was divided into two parts, Communist North Vietnam and non-Communist South Vietnam. National elections to unify the country were scheduled for 1956. But when 1956 rolled around, South Vietnam refused to take part in the elections because it was afraid that North Vietnam would win. At once war between the two Vietnams broke out. The Soviet Union and China sent supplies to North Vietnam, whereas the United States sent supplies and military advisers to South Vietnam. (In 1961 the United States began sending troops as well.)

In 1959 the South Vietnamese government plotted with a local official in Cambodia to overthrow Sihanouk. The plot was discovered and the official was executed. It turned out that the U.S. government had been involved in the plot. Sihanouk was furious.

In the meantime Communist China lost no opportunity to build a closer relationship with Sihanouk. In addition, it seemed to Sihanouk that North Vietnam would eventually defeat South Vietnam. So in 1963 Sihanouk decided to tilt toward the Communist side. He declared he would no longer accept economic and military aid from the United States. Two years later he went even further. He broke diplomatic relations with the United States and gave the Vietminh[4] the right to set up bases in Cambodia from which to supply their soldiers in South Vietnam.

While these events were taking place Sihanouk was encountering serious domestic problems. As a result of his educational policies hundreds of thousands of Khmers were graduating from elementary and high school. Unfortunately, there weren't enough government and other white-collar jobs to go round. To make matters worse, world prices for such Cambodian agricultural exports as rice and rubber kept falling. In addition, farmers in Cambodia's northeast were smuggling their rice into Vietnam to avoid paying export taxes. When the Cambodian army attempted to stop the smuggling, the farmers revolted. The army put down the revolt with great brutality, killing

---

4. **Vietminh** a political group that fought for Vietnam's independence over French rule

some ten thousand farmers in the process. In response the Communist-led Khmer Rouge began waging guerrilla[5] warfare against the army.

By 1970 Sihanouk's one-man rule was in deep trouble. Educated Khmers were unhappy because of high unemployment. Farmers were unhappy because of high taxes. Business people were unhappy because Cambodia was not receiving economic aid from the United States. Army officials were unhappy because of the Vietminh bases in northeast Cambodia. And the influence of the Khmer Rouge was growing.

A Coup d'État

Ironically, one of Sihanouk's most loyal supporters helped overthrow the prince in 1970. General Lon Nol, the head of Cambodia's army, had been appointed prime minister in 1966. It was Lon Nol who was responsible for suppressing the farm revolt that broke out the following year. In late 1969 Lon Nol went to France for medical treatment, leaving the government in the hands of Sihanouk's cousin, Sisowath Sirik Matak.

In January 1970 Sihanouk also went to France for medical treatment. Tense and overweight, he was suffering from diabetes. No sooner had he left than Sirik Matak began denationalizing Cambodia's industries. He also started an intense press campaign against the Vietminh.

The next month Lon Nol returned from France. By this time the Cambodian army was almost ready to move against Sihanouk. In February anti-Vietnamese riots broke out in Phnom Penh. Sirik Matak then gave Lon Nol an ultimatum. Either join with him in overthrowing Sihanouk or be shot at dawn. Lon Nol agreed to join Sirik Matak. On March 18 the National Assembly abolished the monarchy and removed Sihanouk as chief of state. . . .

Cambodia Since 1979

The establishment of the People's Republic of Kampuchea (PRK) with the help of a Vietnamese army was welcomed at home but not abroad. Most Cambodians reacted with "stunned relief." In some villages they turned on their former rulers and killed all the Khmer

---

5. **guerrilla** armed bands of fighters

Rouge they could find. Cambodians who had been resettled by the Khmer Rouge began returning to their cities and villages.

However, China, the United States, and Thailand did not like the political change. All three nations called it "unprovoked aggression" on the part of Vietnam. China feared a stronger, expanding Vietnam on its southern border, especially since Vietnam was an ally of the Soviet Union. The United States was still smarting from its defeat in the Vietnam War and wanted to harass its former enemy. Thailand had been competing with Vietnam for control of Cambodia since the end of the Angkorean Empire.

Accordingly, in February 1979 China invaded Vietnam with some 250,000 troops. The Chinese were going "to teach Vietnam a lesson." Instead the Vietnamese inflicted such heavy losses on the Chinese that they withdrew after only three weeks of fighting. However, the Chinese government—with American approval—sent a steady supply of weapons to the Khmer Rouge in northwestern Cambodia and eastern Thailand. China also voted to let the Khmer Rouge keep Cambodia's seat in the United Nations. So, too, did the United States, which also blocked all humanitarian[6] aid to Cambodia.

For its part Thailand provided a haven for the Khmer Rouge. In addition, some 100,000 Thai workers moved into the part of Cambodia that was under Khmer Rouge control. There they worked either in the local mines, digging for rubies and sapphires, or in the forests, logging teak and other hardwoods. The gems and lumber were then sold in Thailand and the money used by the Khmer Rouge to purchase additional weapons. Ironically, at the same time Thailand continued sheltering almost 350,000 Cambodians who had fled their homeland to escape the Pol Pot[7] regime. These refugees lived in camps along the border between the two countries.

Rebuilding Cambodia

Vietnam kept its army in Cambodia throughout the 1980s. In addition, several hundred thousand Vietnamese civilians settled in the country. Most had formerly lived in Cambodia but had been driven out by Lon Nol. Now they resumed their previous occupations.

---

6. **humanitarian** concerned with the well-being of people
7. **Pol Pot** Khmer political leader (1975–79) whose policies were responsible for the mass evacuation of cities, country-wide poverty, and the deaths of over a million people

At first the PRK government tried to follow the Communist economic principles being followed in Vietnam. But it soon became clear that most Cambodians wanted nothing to do with anything resembling "Pol Pot time." The Cambodians, like the Vietnamese, also found that a command economy controlled by the government did not produce many consumer goods. Accordingly, the PRK government gradually shifted toward a free enterprise economy, especially after Hun Sen became prime minister in 1985. (Like Heng Samrin, Hun Sen was a former member of the Khmer Rouge who had broken with Pol Pot, taken refuge in Vietnam, and returned to Cambodia in 1979.) The PRK allowed private ownership of land and real estate. Collective farms were replaced by family farms. Private stores, restaurants, repair shops, and small factories opened for business. State-owned enterprises were privatized[8] or sold to private individuals. There were social changes, too. Schools reopened, and Buddhism once again became the country's official religion.

At the same time the corruption that had been widespread under Sihanouk and Lon Nol sprang up again, especially in Phnom Penh. Many people with government connections became rich through smuggling or speculating in currency. Bribery was commonplace. Patients even had to pay to be admitted into "free" hospitals.

Nevertheless, everyday life within Cambodia was far better under the People's Republic of Kampuchea than it had been under the Khmer Rouge. Political stability,[9] though, remained as hard to achieve as ever.

An Ongoing Civil War

In 1979 the Khmer Rouge had vowed to continue fighting for control of Cambodia. Despite its murderous rule, the Khmer Rouge managed to gain some support. How? By combining gifts with threats. The Khmer Rouge gave away rich farmland in the northwest to some of the nation's poorer farmers. Naturally, the new landowners were grateful. At the same time the Khmer Rouge terrorized the local inhabitants, warning them that, "When the Vietnamese are gone, every well will hold one hundred bodies." The local people responded by supplying the Khmer Rouge with food, information, and even recruits.

---

8. **privatized** changed from government ownership to private ownership
9. **political stability** orderly changes in government

The Khmer Rouge was very clever in its political propaganda. It presented itself as the symbol of Cambodian nationalist resistance to foreign control—in this case, Vietnam. This was an appealing argument, especially since many Cambodians hated the Vietnamese. Even Prince Sihanouk said in 1989, "The Khmer Rouge are tigers. But I would rather be eaten by a Khmer Rouge tiger than by a Vietnamese crocodile."

As for Sihanouk, he, too, opposed the PRK government. The prince had returned to Cambodia after the fall of Lon Nol and had agreed to serve as head of state in the Khmer Rouge government. However, the Communists treated him with great contempt and kept him more or less under house arrest. They even murdered five of his children and fourteen other relatives. When the Communists fled from Phnom Penh in 1979, Sihanouk fled also, to his former sanctuary[10] of Beijing.

In 1982, pressed by China and the United States, Sihanouk formed a coalition government-in-exile with himself as president. The vice-president was Son Sann, a conservative who was backed by many Cambodian refugees in Thailand. Over the next seven years the coalition waged a guerrilla war against the People's Republic of Kampuchea. But little was accomplished. Sihanouk resigned from and then rejoined the coalition several times. Son Sann's group quarreled internally. Khmer Rouge soldiers fought against Sihanouk's supporters as well as against the Vietnamese. And the Cambodian people suffered and died.

In 1987 Hun Sen approached Sihanouk and suggested that the prince and the Phnom Penh government form an alliance.[11] It was the best means of protecting Cambodia against the Khmer Rouge, argued Hun Sen. The PRK would supply troops, while Sihanouk would supply respectability and thus enable the PRK to obtain help from other countries. But the United States opposed the alliance because it did not want the Vietnamese-supported Hun Sen government to be recognized internationally. So the agreement fell through.

---

10. **sanctuary** place that provides protection
11. **alliance** union or association

The United Nations Makes Peace

Real changes started happening in 1989. That year Vietnam withdrew almost all its troops from the People's Republic of Kampuchea, now renamed Cambodia. This reassured China, which no longer felt it had to support the Khmer Rouge against the Hun Sen government. In addition, China had created an international scandal in the spring, when it sent troops and tanks into Beijing's Tiananmen Square to break up a peaceful pro-democracy demonstration. Hundreds of students and workers had been killed. Now China wanted to appear in a better light. Helping to end the civil war in Cambodia seemed to be one way to accomplish this.

The United States likewise changed its policy. In 1985, as a result of publicity about "the killing fields," the United States Congress passed a law prohibiting military aid to the Khmer Rouge. Yet the United States Central Intelligence Agency (CIA) continued supplying Sihanouk and Son Sann with materials that ended up in Khmer Rouge hands. Congressional pressure against this policy kept building. Finally, the U.S. government agreed to open talks with Vietnam about bringing peace to Cambodia.

In January 1990 the five permanent members of the United Nations Security Council—the United States, China, the Soviet Union, Great Britain, and France—drafted a peace plan. In its final form, the plan called for elections to be held in 1993 under UN supervision. The UN would run Cambodia until then. A cease-fire was declared, and the four factions competing for power—the Hun Sen government, the Khmer Rouge, the Sihanoukists, and Son Sann—agreed to reduce their armies and weapons by 70 percent. The 350,000 or so refugees in Thailand were to be returned to Cambodia.

The peace plan was signed in October 1991. For the first time in a generation it seemed as if civil war in Cambodia might become a thing of the past.

Linda Crew

from
Children of
the River

*Some refugees from the continuing warfare in
Cambodia were able to return to their villages and
their traditional occupations during times of peace.
Others who had been forced to immigrate to distant
countries have learned new ways of life and new
occupations. In this excerpt from another novel
about Cambodian experiences, the main character,
Sundara, and her uncle's family have to flee to the
United States to save their lives.*

April 17, 1975

For a brief time, it seemed the New Year had brought good fortune
to the household of Tep Naro in the Cambodian village of Réam: a
fat-cheeked new daughter born to his wife, Soka.

The birth itself had not been an easy one, however, and Naro and
Soka were glad their young niece Sundara had come down from
Phnom Penh to help.

On the day after the birth Sundara sat rocking the new baby in
the wooden swing on the front porch. The afternoon air was soft and
warm; a pleasant breeze wafted up from the gulf. Nuzzling the baby,
she breathed in the sweet newborn smell. Such a nice plump little
body. Such a thick thatch of black hair.

In the hammock, Sundara's six-year-old cousin, Ravy, lay nibbling
leftover sticky rice cakes and entertaining his little brother Pon with
a boat he'd made of knotted straw.

A sad love song played on the radio and Sundara kept time, lazily dangling her rubber thong[1] from her toe, thinking of Chamroeun, the boy she'd left back in the city two weeks ago.

"I want to go fight the Communists," he'd told her that last night in Phnom Penh, the night before her father had spirited her through the teeming,[2] refugee-choked boulevards to the airport. Hearing those words as the shells from the Communist guns screamed at the city's edge had terrified her. But now it seemed only a bad dream. Here, safe in her relatives' fishing village, lulled by the rustling of the coconut palms, she could almost imagine this as simply another vacation. The war that had dominated their lives seemed so far away, so unreal . . .

When the baby fussed, Sundara jiggled her, clicking her tongue as she'd seen the other women do. This seemed to calm the little one. Sundara smiled. She was beginning to feel quite capable, much older than thirteen. "Don't worry," she whispered to the baby, whom she had already grown to love, "I'll take care of you."

Suddenly the radio music stopped for an announcement . . . something about a new government. Then a terse[3] exchange, a brief commotion. Then, nothing. Sundara shifted the baby to one arm and turned the dial.

"That's odd," she murmured to Ravy. "It's gone dead."

A moment later two men hurried past the house. Then, a panicky family.

Sundara rose. "What's happening?" she called. "Where's everyone going?"

"Get out! Get away! The Communists! The Khmer Rouge![4] They've taken Phnom Penh and they're coming here!"

The Communists! Hot fear burned her chest. She whirled and ran into the main room.

"Grandmother! Younger Aunt! Wake up! The Khmer Rouge are coming! Everyone's running away!"

Soka moaned, more in pain than alarm. "What does Naro say?"

"Naro's not here! He's still at work."

Soka shifted on her wooden bed. "I can't go anyway. Not *now*."

---

1. **thong** sandal held to the foot by a strap between the toes
2. **teeming** filled to overflowing
3. **terse** short, having no extra words
4. **Khmer Rouge** radical political organization in Cambodia

Grandmother peered out the window. "Just wait for Naro, child. My son is the head of this family. I'm sure he'll tell us this is nothing."

Clutching the baby, Sundara paced the house. The servant girl had fled down the back steps, leaving supper to burn. How much time did the rest of them have?

The trickle of people in the street became a stream.

Watching them, Grandmother sniffed. "I, for one, don't plan to leave my home just because the government might change hands once again. What has that got to do with an old woman like me?"

Brave words, Sundara thought, but Grandmother had not seen the billboards all over Phnom Penh, the hideous picture that warned what the Khmer Rouge would do if they came to power. . . .

"Don't just stand there, you foolish women!" Naro jumped off his roaring motorcycle, let it fall in the dusty yard. "Haven't you heard?" He hauled the two-wheeled cart from under the house. "Throw our things in this. Now!"

Sundara dashed into the house. Laying the baby on a mat, she tossed clothes into a satchel.[5] "We're leaving, Younger Aunt."

"But I can't!" Soka protested. "It's impossible!"

Naro ran in. "Up, Soka! Hurry!" He flung open the teakwood chest, rummaged for a packet at the bottom.

"Are you crazy, Husband? Have you forgotten? I just had a baby! I'm still bleeding. If you make me go now, I will die!"

Sweat beaded his forehead. "If we stay, we will *all* die. Everyone who worked for the United States must get out *now!*" He turned on Sundara and Grandmother. "You two, grab that basket of dried fish, the small gas stove . . ." He scooped Soka from her bed and bore her down the steps.

The baby fussed frantically at the commotion. Sundara snatched up her checkered *krama* and lashed the red-faced bundle to her breast, then rushed through the house grabbing dishes, food, mats. Just one thing more. The parasol.[6] Her chest clutched tight. *Phnom Penh! Oh, God, what about her family, what about Chamroeun—No. No time for that now . . .*

"You're killing me!" Soka was screaming down in the yard. "We haven't even had the childbirth ceremonies yet. We cannot leave

---

5. **satchel** small bag
6. **parasol** lightweight umbrella used as a sunshade

without purifying[7] the house!"

Grandmother tugged at Naro's sleeve. "She's right, my son. The spirits won't like it if—"

"Shut up! Both of you! Now hurry!"

Pon burst out crying.

Sundara threw everything into the cart and plopped the toddler on a sack of rice. She seized a cart handle and Grandmother, in a daze, did the same. Together they shoved the heavy contraption[8] after Naro, who staggered ahead toward the wharf under Soka's sobbing weight. Behind them, Ravy struggled to keep up, bravely lugging the pot of supper they'd yanked from the fire as an afterthought.

"Where are we going?" he kept calling.

No one answered.

People crowded on the pier with their squalling children and hastily gathered possessions, stumbling in panic up the gangplank to a large freighter. A few men rolled motorcycles on board; one family pushed a refrigerator. All was shouting and confusion. Where were they going and for how long? Who should be let on? Who must be left behind? Somehow Naro knew the right people: his family would be allowed to board.

Night was coming on fast. The wind whipped Sundara's hair about her face as she gripped the baby in her *krama* with one arm, balanced Pon on her opposite hip and, swept by the mass of people, began the long, sloping climb up the gangplank to the ship.

For hours, it seemed, she had been picking her way among the people crammed together on the hot metal deck, trying to shield the baby from the blazing sun with her bleached-out parasol. Three weeks they'd been on the sea, and Soka was ill. Sundara had been left to care for the little one alone.

She scanned the crowd. Surely there was one nursing mother among these hundreds of people, a woman who could help her. Ah! Over there, sitting by the motorcycle . . .

Sundara bowed awkwardly before the young mother and her child. "Excuse me, please. My aunt is very sick and her milk has dried up. Now her little one grows weak too." She pulled back the blue-checkered

---

7. **purifying** making pure or cleaning
8. **contraption** device

krama. "See how strange and dried out her skin is? Look. Even her soft spot sinks in."

The woman winced, then averted her eyes. She held her own baby a little closer.

Sundara licked the salt from her cracked lips. "I was wondering . . . could you . . . ?"

"I'm sorry," the woman whispered, "I would, but . . . Oh, this is all so terrible. I'm not getting enough to drink myself. Soon I'm afraid I won't have milk for my own."

Sundara nodded, swallowing hard. Everyone had the same story. Their own families had to come first. She covered the baby and moved on. Heaven protect her, the baby grew lighter by the moment, her life running out in diarrhea that stained Sundara's cotton sarong in reeking brown streaks. How limp she was, and so silent . . .

Oh God, what to do?

She went down to the hold where they guarded the donated supplies and found it crowded with people pleading for extra shares. She pushed into the weary crush. Breathless with the heat, she finally squeezed through to one of the men in charge.

"Our baby is so sick. Can you give me something for her?"

"Everyone's sick," he replied impatiently, showing bad teeth. His breath stank. "Everyone wants something extra. There's not enough extra for all seven hundred!"

Sundara shut her eyes, faint with disappointment and lack of air.

"For the love of heaven," said a woman. "Can't you even give her an extra packet of milk?" Her voice softened. "Poor child. No grown-ups to help you?"

"They all have the seasickness," Sundara whispered.

The man's mouth twisted. "Well, here then." Grudgingly, he shoved a packet at her.

Tears squeezed from the corners of her eyes.

"*Now* what's the matter?" he demanded.

"Thank you. I'm grateful, but . . . I think that's partly what made her sick, because before I had to mix milk in water without boiling it first." She took a deep breath, gathering courage. "I need medicine."

"Medicine! Do you think this is a hospital? Do I look like a doctor? I wouldn't know what to give you if I had it." He glanced around. "That Thai ship donated these. Sugar water or something." He held up a glass bottle of clear liquid. "Although I don't know what they expect us to do with them since this is for putting in the veins and we don't have any needles."

"I'll take it," Sundara said quickly. It was liquid; it looked clean. She had to try something.

"All right. But one thing—we don't need any more diseases than we've got. If that baby dies, throw it overboard right away."

What! Throw the baby—Horrible man. She snatched the bottle and struggled out through the press of people, holding the little bundle tighter than ever. This baby *couldn't* die. She wouldn't let her. She would do anything. She would find a way to feed her. She would pray to God, promise to shave off all her long hair in gratitude if only the child would live. . . .

Nothing had changed back at their tiny section of the deck. Ravy huddled dejectedly with Pon, whose eyes were taking on the same sunken look as his baby sister's. The three grown-ups sprawled against the sack of rice, oblivious to the beating sun. Sundara squinted upward, hand shading her eyes. The tarp[9] the ship people tried to rig had been ripped away by the hot wind. No shade, and nothing she could do about it. Well, she could at least try to clean up their patch of deck. She pulled a sarong from their satchel and swabbed at the new vomit. Hurry. Mustn't let it bake on the hot metal. Oh, no! Now little Pon had diarrhea too.

"Help me, Ravy." She propped Pon against the suitcase and handed Ravy the baby. She unpeeled the bottle's silver seal and yanked out the stopper, dividing the liquid between a cup and the baby bottle she'd begged from another family. She handed Ravy the cup for Pon, quickly looking away, unable to bear those big, questioning six-year-old eyes.

"Now, you must drink," she coaxed, cradling the baby again. "Please, *please* drink." But the tiny head fell back from the bottle. "Oh, Little One, can't you swallow? No, no, don't let it dribble away . . ."

September 7, 1979

The third-floor classroom window was open, allowing a wispy thistle seed to float in on a breath of late summer air. Sundara clenched her hands on her desk and watched the spinning puff drift by. When you

---

9. tarp sheet of durable material used for protecting objects

saw one of these, you could make a wish. An American girl who worked beside her in the strawberry fields had told her that. Sundara closed her eyes. *How I wish I had not written that poem.*

Every muscle in her body was tense. She never dreamed Mrs. Cathcart would read these first English papers aloud.

"In conclusion," the teacher read from a student's paper, "let us choose our own lunch menus. A lot less food would end up in the garbage if we did."

"Yay," came one listless voice. This was the sixth paper on cafeteria food, and only one—the blond boy's—had been truly funny. The students were sinking ever lower in their hard wooden chairs. . . .

"And now I'd like to share a very special piece of work by Sundara Sovann." Mrs. Cathcart smiled at Sundara. "If she doesn't object."

I do object! Sundara longed to cry. But of course she couldn't. Deny a teacher's request? Impossible. She glanced behind her. Thirty pairs of eyes bored into her, waiting. True, one girl had written about her cat dying, but the rest of these eyes belonged to a puzzling group of people who had chosen video games, school dress codes, and football team conduct rules as topics that concerned them most deeply. Sundara sighed. Even now, four years after leaving Cambodia, she could not seem to understand the Americans.

Lowering her eyes, focusing once more on her scratched, damp-palmed hands, she finally nodded.

> "We are lost, we are the lonely
> So far from our beloved land
> We are the children of the Mekong
> Who will not see that mighty river again
> O Kampuchea
> The blood of our people
> Has stained you
> The bones of our people
> Lie in unmarked graves
> But the love of the ancient Khmers
> Will live in our hearts
> We will not forget you
> Even from this new place
> On the far side
> Of the earth."

Silence. Endless silence. She did not look up as the teacher slipped the offending paper into her view. *Very good*, Mrs. Cathcart had written in red pencil, but the praise was small compensation for this embarrassment. Why hadn't she written about something safe, like the others?

She couldn't wait to get away when the bell rang, away from all those staring eyes. Threading through the crowds, she hurried down the two flights of stairs to the girls' locker room to dress for PE, her last class of the day.

"Sundara, what's wrong?" It was Kelly, her chemistry lab partner, peering at her. Kelly's glasses made her eyes look huge.

"Not'ing," Sundara said. She could never master the *t-h* sound.

"Come on. You're acting like somebody's after you."

Sundara forced herself to smile calmly as she gathered her long black hair into her fist and snapped a clip around it. "Not'ing is wrong." She and Kelly had been friendly since the seventh grade, when they'd met at the church that sponsored Sundara's family. Even so, Sundara had never spoken of her homesickness to Kelly. Not to anyone. When they'd first come to Oregon, she had been too busy learning to live in America, and the kind ones, like Kelly, had been too busy trying to teach her.

Perhaps because of her faltering[10] English, no one had tried, at first, to coax out her story, no one except that boy with pimply red skin. "How many people did you see get killed?" he'd ask her, eyes glittering. She shuddered, glad he was at her old high school. She would have hated to have him hear her poem.

"So how's it going?" Kelly asked. "Finding your way around okay?"

Sundara nodded. She hadn't been happy when she learned that moving to a new house would mean enrolling at the other high school. She was just getting to know people at Kennedy. But it would be all right. Changing schools was nothing compared to changing countries.

Out on the field, she kicked the soccer ball with the others, but she couldn't concentrate. Now, because of her putting those words on paper, far too many people knew her thoughts. Which was worse, to walk around with everything held inside so that no one really knew you? Or to have these feelings exposed to the whole world? Her aunt

---

10. **faltering** uncertain

and uncle would be most displeased if they knew of this. Hadn't they warned her against telling their troubles or sounding ungrateful for their new life here? Hadn't they insisted the first English words they learned must be "Thank you very much" and "Very happy to be here"?

Even after PE, she was still so distracted, she stood waiting for the bus by the curb a minute before remembering her aunt had sent her with the station wagon that morning so she could hurry home for tomato picking.

She turned into the subdivision where their small house sat in a row with the others, the young, twiglike trees not yet large enough to soften the raw newness of the neighborhood. *I hope Soka won't notice I'm late*, she thought. They had to keep to American time now. Three-thirty meant three-thirty exactly.

But when Soka flung open the door and ran out onto the driveway, she was clearly upset by something more important than Sundara's being five minutes late. "Niece!" she cried in Khmer. "Quickly! Come see this letter. Grandmother and I can do nothing but weep all day!" She hurried Sundara in, hardly giving her time to place her shoes on the mat by the door.

Sundara set her books on the kitchen counter and followed her aunt into the living room. Grandmother crouched on a straw mat, her close-cropped gray head bowed in despair, touching the paper in question as if trying to decipher[11] the strange markings with her gnarled fingers alone.

Soka took the letter from her and thrust it at Sundara, who by now was trembling in sick anticipation, her mind whirling with the awful possibilities.

"Will you boys turn down that foolishness?" Soka called to her sons in the next room. "We cannot think." The hysterical cheering of a TV game show snapped off. Silence.

Swallowing hard, Sundara unfolded the paper. *The Office of the United Nations High Commissioner for Refugees, Thailand.* News of her parents, her brother and sister? No, scanning the brief lines, she saw only the name of another aunt, Soka's sister Valinn, who, at the end of the last dry season, had scrambled down Khao-I-Dang mountain into a Thai border camp and collapsed in a malarial stupor.[12]

---

11. **decipher** make out the meaning of something
12. **malarial stupor** partly conscious condition caused by malaria

Sundara let out a tentative breath. "Younger Aunt, why are you so upset? It's not the news we want, but there is still hope, isn't there? It says here they need more information before we can sponsor her. They want us to—"

"But look. *Look*." Soka jabbed a finger at the crackly onionskin paper. "I've taken this to Prom Kea to tell me what the English says. And you see? 'Do not contact us again on this case.' Who can we turn to if not the United Nations? Prom Kea is telling his friends about this too. Everyone is very upset."

"Younger Aunt—"

"Do they expect us to simply forget our families? My own sister? Oiee!"

"Younger Aunt, do you see this word? *Hesitate*. It says, 'Please do not hesitate to contact us again." It means just the opposite of what you thought. It's all right to write them more letters. They *want us* to."

Soka's round face went blank, then lit with a broad, embarrassed smile. "Oh!" She put her palms to her cheeks. "Oh, I was so scared." She dropped to a squat next to Grandmother. "It's a mistake," she said into the old woman's ear. "The United Nations will still try to help us." She allowed herself a moment to enjoy the relief, then jumped up. "That Prom Kea! He thinks he knows English so well! But then, I am too glad about this to be angry. Quick, Niece, change your clothes. There's some cold corn for you in the kitchen." Then she called to the boys. "Ravy, Pon, come now! Grandmother, are you ready? We will pick many tomatoes tonight and send the money we earn to Valinn. Hurry, hurry, or the Lam family will pick the whole field before we get there."

Perfect weather for picking Mr. Bonner's fall raspberries and cherry tomatoes: warm, sunny, and dry. Sundara crouched over her row, her quick fingers stripping the small orange tomatoes from the vines. It hadn't taken them long to harvest the small berry patch, and the tomatoes were now thunking into the plastic buckets with a steady intensity.

"Pon!" Sundara called, brushing away the mosquito that tentatively tickled her lower lip. "I need an empty one."

Her six-year-old cousin picked his way through the scratchy vines with another cardboard flat in which he'd placed a dozen Styrofoam pint boxes. Sundara spilled the bucket of tomatoes into the flat.

"Fore!" On the other side of the blackberry and poison oak thickets that lined the fence, golfers strolled about the adjacent course, playing their odd game. To Sundara, the women golfers always seemed so brown and wrinkled. Americans certainly had funny ideas about what looked nice. She had even seen one blond girl pruning berry vines for Mr. Bonner in a bathing suit! Her skin was burned a deep brown, but she only seemed concerned with her nose, which was smeared with some kind of thick white paste. Sundara stood and retied the strings of her broad-brimmed straw hat. She did not want the sun to darken her skin, and avoided even the late afternoon rays.

She stooped back to work, slapping another mosquito on her cheek. "Here's a full one," she called. Ten-year-old Ravy carried the loaded flat to Mr. Bonner's truck, where Grandmother sat dreaming and sorting out the occasional bad tomato.

Sundara's fingers flew. This was the last crop of the season and the best money-maker of all, an opportunity Soka did her best to guard. If all the refugees they knew who wanted to work came to Mr. Bonner's small farm, no single family would earn much at all. Sundara had often heard Soka turn vague when the others tried to coax it out of her.

"Ah, the cherry tomatoes again," they would say with more than a trace of resentment. "And where can you possibly be picking raspberries in September? Are you trying to make your first million this year?"

Soka would help these others if she could, Sundara knew, but their own family had to come first. As long as Valinn was still in Khao-I-Dang they had to send money to her. And what of the others in Kampuchea itself, the ones from whom they'd had no word? If they were alive, they might be needing money to bribe an escape. So Soka kept news of work to herself. And since Mr. Bonner couldn't communicate well with most of the Asians, she exerted a fair amount of control over how many families came to pick.

Tonight, only the Lam family worked alongside them. The Lams had come to America just last year after escaping Vietnam by boat. They were Chinese, and as Soka always pointed out with a grudging admiration, the Chinese could practically smell money to be made. You could not expect to keep work secret from them. Lam Ming, the father, picked with admirable speed, even though Sundara thought it must hurt his pride to do this work at all, having managed his own wholesale produce company in his homeland.

Faster, *faster*, Sundara urged herself, working steadily to the clank of the plastic bucket handles, the drumming of tomatoes on the bucket bottoms, the distant chug of Mr. Bonner's tractor as he disked under an early corn patch.

At six Sundara's Uncle Naro appeared, having parked his new Ford near the Bonners' house rather than dirty it on the dusty farm road. He had changed from office to work clothes, and carried a sack of Big Macs for the children.

Soka glanced up just long enough to point out the next unpicked row to her husband. Naro kicked off his thongs, smoothly curled into a crouch, and proceeded to strip tomatoes into his bucket like a well-oiled machine.

Sundara sat down next to Grandmother. She would have to eat quickly. It didn't seem right, taking too much time when Soka refused to stop even for a minute. But how Sundara's body longed for rest! She could have laid herself in the dirt and been asleep instantly.

"Are you hungry, Grandmother?"

The old woman sniffed. "Not for that pig slop."

None of the grown-ups cared for American food, and they hated the idea of eating in the middle of such dirty work. They preferred to go hungry until they could bathe and eat something decent. But Sundara was ravenous,[13] and as for Ravy, he loved burgers and fries. He ate them every chance he got, and laughed at Soka's warning: "Watch out! You'll start to smell like an American!" Now he slurped down his Coke, dumped the ice, and trotted out to fill the paper cup with wayward golf balls, which he planned to sell.

Grandmother sighed. "I never thought I'd live to see my family work the dirt like peasants."

"Uncle says you loved the garden in Réam."

"A garden is one thing. To slave in someone else's field is another."

"This is hard work, but surely it isn't slavery, Grandmother. We *are* earning money."

"Rubbish! Keeping your knees busy for someone else. How I miss the warm Cambodian sun, my loom in the pleasant shade of the

---

13. **ravenous** extremely hungry

house. Why did they ever force me to come here?"

Sundara did not try to answer. No one could make Naro's mother understand that she was dreaming of a Kampuchea that no longer existed. If she'd stayed behind, she would have seen real slavery. If she'd lived.

"Any day now they'll be locking me in one of those terrible nursing homes."

Sundara sighed. She had heard this so often, it no longer moved her as it had at first. "You know your son will never lock you away, Grandmother. Hasn't he promised?"

"Perhaps a promise doesn't mean the same thing in America. Nothing else does."

Sundara stood, carefully gathering the paper wrappings and stuffing them in the sack. Thank the heavens the season was nearly over. They had begun in June with strawberries and picked every crop in the valley that needed swift and careful human hands for harvest. A whole ton of boysenberries, three tons of pole beans. Sometimes the crops overlapped. One day they had come home exhausted from blueberry picking to find the phone ringing. It was Mr. Bonner. Did they want to pick tomatoes that evening? Wordlessly, they'd piled back into the car.

Tonight they picked until dusk. Their practiced hands could find the little tomatoes with their eyes closed, but they had to quit when they could no longer tell the properly pale orange fruits from the green or overripe red.

Sundara was already at the truck when Soka picked her way, barefoot, out of the tangled rows, weighed down by a stack of three flats. She set them on the wooden pallet with a grunt and straightened up, bracing her back, rubbing her dirty sleeve across her forehead. Strands of black hair had escaped from the knot at the back of her neck and were sticking to her cheeks. She sighed deeply. Then, noticing Sundara watching her, she returned one of those long, searching looks that always made Sundara uneasy.

"What do you think, Niece? Would your mother call me 'little pampered lady' now as she used to?"

Sundara hesitated. Was Soka feeling proud or sad? She answered honestly. "I think not, Younger Aunt."

She busied herself counting the flats and helping Mr. Bonner load them. Fifty for their family. They had done well.

"You people sure can pick," Mr. Bonner said, stacking the last flats on the truck.

"We pick more tomorrow?" Soka asked in her broken but confident English.

Sundara wondered where her aunt found the will to sound so eager for more work when a moment before she seemed ready to collapse.

"Well," Mr. Bonner said, considering, "how about Sunday? My wholesalers won't take anything on Saturday night."

"Okay, Sunday. But first have to go to church." Soka insisted the family present themselves regularly at the First Presbyterian Church, which had sponsored them. "Pray to Buddha, pray to our ancestors, or pray to Jesus Christ," she always said. "It's all the same anyway. The important thing is to go and show our gratitude."

"Do you want to call some of the other families, then?" Mr. Bonner asked.

"Oh, we pick all," Soka put in quickly. "No problem." She knew the words to say to Mr. Bonner. Useful phrases such as "Those other people not pick clean. We pick clean." Or "We happy to start more early in the morning if you want."

"We also wish to pick," said Chun-Ling, the Lam daughter who did most of the interpreting for her family.

"Yes, Lam family, too, of course," Soka said, nodding deferentially[14] at the girl's mother. Sundara and Chun-Ling exchanged glances. Neither had made any effort to become friends, but there was a certain understanding between them. They were, as the Americans put it, in the same boat.

"I guess I'll see *you* tomorrow, then, right?" Mr. Bonner said to Sundara.

Sundara nodded, proud. She was the one he'd singled out to sell his produce at the Saturday farmers' market.

They plodded up the parallel ruts of the dirt road, passing through alternating pockets of warm and cool air, wispy puffs of haze forming where the sun-heated earth met the chill of the coming night. Sundara carried Pon in her aching arms, his head nodding sleepily against her shoulder. A few stars blinked, but before they could brighten, the moon loomed above the eastern treetops, glowing orange through the field smoke.

---

14. **deferentially** in a respectful manner

Soka stooped to gather some tender young pigweed she had spotted earlier. She liked to scold Mr. Bonner about all the good food he grew without trying and then never bothered to harvest.

"Listen," she whispered, standing up, holding the greens. "What's that sound?"

They stopped, and in the quiet punctuated only by the chirping crickets, Sundara heard a distant roar. It died away, then rose again, coming from the direction of town. They all looked west, back across the Willamette River, where the lights of town paled the sky.

"I know!" Ravy cried. "It's the high school football game! The fans are going wild!"

"Soka, this son of ours! He's so American."

"I know. How do you think I feel, always having a child explain things to me?" Her voice wavered between annoyance and pride.

"Odd, isn't it?" Naro said. "How the sound carries over the fields."

The football game, Sundara thought. That's probably what the rest of the students were doing tonight. She shifted Pon in her arms and followed the others along the soft dirt road.

. . . He opened his notebook, flipped through the pages to some jotted questions. "Okay . . . what was it like, living in the middle of a war?"

"Oohh . . . Hard to say. I cannot remember my country without a war. But when I'm small in Phnom Penh, it seem far away. The grown-up keep talking how something bad gonna happen, but I don't pay any attention. By the end, though, no one can ignore. My school close down because of the bombing just when I supposed to take my examination for the *lycée*, and—"

"*Lycée?*"

"Oh, that French. It mean like a high school. Anyway, I study so hard for the test. In my country, you not pass this, no more school for you unless you are a high-up person and your father can pay for private school. My father cannot pay, but he want me to get a good education, so I study hard. Then they shoot the rockets and I don't get to take my test! I get so mad! After that is the long vacation. But all the road into Phnom Penh are blocked so we cannot go down to the sea at Réam. Cannot go anywhere. Cannot even go to the cinema. Just stay home and listen to my mother complaining how the food cost more every time she go to the market. It's like crazy inflation, you know?"

"But you never really saw any fighting?"

She smiled grimly. "Only in our house." She touched her fingers to her lips. "But I shouldn't tell about that." She took a small bite of her sandwich. Surprising, the way the words were pouring out. English words. This American boy had done nothing but smile at her encouragingly and here she was, putting into English things she'd never spoken of before in any language.

"Why shouldn't you talk about it?" Jonathan persisted.

She frowned. "Not right to tell our family trouble . . . " He seemed to be waiting for her to go on. She hesitated, then recklessly plunged ahead. "Just that everybody get so cranky, you know? My father a teacher at another *lycée*, so he home all the time. This the hot season. Everybody kind of pick on each other . . . I'm sorry now. I feel bad when I think how I talk to them."

Jonathan smiled. "Somehow it's hard for me to picture you as a rotten kid."

"It is true. My mother say I'm sassy." She tilted her head. "I'm a different person now, though. Like I already die and now I am reborn."

Jonathan gave her a startled look. She flushed.

Perhaps this was the danger, she thought, in talking to Americans. You constantly risked stepping over some invisible boundary, saying something they'd find odd. . . .

"Okay . . . " Jonathan looked up. "Do you think it's possible that people watching war coverage on TV see more bombing and stuff than the people actually there do?"

She blinked at the change of subject. "I don't know. We don't have a TV in Cambodia. Do they show a lot of bomb?"

"Here, they did," Jonathan said. "Every night."

"What I see," she told him, "is what the war does to the people. Before, Phnom Penh is a beautiful city, but by the end it's crowded with refugees from the countryside. You know, they make a tent on all the sidewalk . . . " She trailed off. Sitting here in the peaceful autumn sunshine, all that seemed so long ago and far away. Did she really want to bring it back? The wretched women fanning clouds of flies from their sick-looking children. The stench of overflowing garbage rotting in the late dry-season heat. You couldn't get that from television. The cratered[15] streets, the rubbled buildings, the people with

---

15. **cratered** marked with bowl-shaped depressions

limbs missing, wounds bound in filthy bandages, crusty with rust-red blood . . .

"The main thing I remember about the Vietnam War," Jonathan said, "is my mother's antiwar petitions. She and my dad got in a big fight because one time she took them to a party for people from the clinic. My dad had just started working there and he was afraid people would get upset."

"And did they?"

"It upset my dad, that's for sure." Jonathan shrugged. "So that's my memory of the war. I didn't really understand what it was all about; I just knew it was something so horrible, Mom had to keep turning the TV off so I wouldn't see it on the news."

Sundara sighed. "My mother doesn't want me to see it either. That's why they keep me home. I never know how bad everything is until I leave."

"I'll bet you're glad you got out when you did, huh?"

She felt the corners of her mouth twitch. Jonathan saw this.

"Look, we don't have to talk about Cambodia, if it's going to make you feel bad."

"I don't mind, if it help you for your report."

"Well, if you're sure." He tapped the *Newsweek* on the top of his stack. "I've already read some about it. Enough to know I'm really glad you got out of there. I mean, I know you miss your home, but from what I've read about the Khmer Rouge being so down on intellectuals, it would have been terrible if you'd stayed. Your dad was a teacher . . . " He shook his head. "Just lucky he got out in time."

"But Jonatan . . . " She laid down her fork carefully. "He doesn't get out."

Jonathan's sloppy joe stopped halfway to his mouth. "What do you mean? I thought—"

"I leave my whole family in Phnom Penh."

He dropped the sandwich onto the tray. "Oh, God, Sundara. I'm *sorry*. I didn't know. When you talked about your family I just assumed . . . "

"No, I come with my aunt and uncle because I'm with them in Réam when Phnom Penh fall down. Maybe I don't explain right before."

He swallowed hard. "So what happened to your parents?"

"I don't know. I hear nothing."

"In all this time?"

She shook her head. "The last day I see my father is when he take me to the airport."

"But that's awful."

She nodded. "My parent send me on the plane to Réam only a couple week before the Khmer Rouge take over. Plane is the only way out because all the road blocked. That's when I see the city all falling apart. The boulevard jam full of bicycle, oxcart, motorcycle, big green soldier truck—everything. All the big, pretty house pile up with sand-bag to protect. I just hang on to my father in the pedicab[16] and stare. I never know until now how bad the war is making everything. I re-member the driver drop us at the taxi station, says, 'Twenty riel.' My father say, 'You crazy! That four time the regular.' He go, 'This war. You not the only one in a hurry to get someplace.' The airport a mess too. Everybody pushing, worried to get out. Then the shell come screaming."

"Right when you were there?"

"Yes! My father throw me on the pavement. My chest burn, I'm so scared. I feel the hot ground shake my face. Then he yank me up, drag me to the plane step. By now I don't want to go at all, just want to stay with my family. I'm crying, but he doesn't listen. I tell him, look, my elbow bleeding and his glasses have a crack, but he just shove me up with the people."

"And you haven't heard anything since then?"

"No. Only the rumor about what happen when the Khmer Rouge take Phnom Penh. A few who escape say the Communist make every-one march into the country to work and many die. Sometime I say to myself, 'Sundara, you may already be *kamprea*.' That mean orphan. A couple day ago we have a holiday, All Soul Day. We pray for everyone who already die. But I don't know who to pray for, because—well, who die and who doesn't?"

After a moment Jonathan shook his head as if he couldn't believe her story. "Leaving without your parents . . . " he said.

"*And* my brother and little sister." She sighed. "And Chamroeun."

"Chamroeun?"

"He a boy I know."

"Boyfriend?"

---

16. **pedicab** a tricycle with a two-seat passenger compartment

She studied her hands. "Kind of like that." She looked up at him again. "Maybe I shouldn't make you sad about this."

For a long time they said nothing. They had both stopped eating. Finally she said, "How many brother and sister do you have?"

"None. I'm it."

"Ah! That too bad!"

He blinked. "There *are* certain advantages to being an only child, you know."

"Oh, forgive? I don't meaning to offend."

"No, that's okay." He laughed. "I guess I'm just not used to people feeling sorry for me. Everybody always acts like I'm the kid with everything."

"But no brother or sister . . . "

He shrugged. "I'm used to it."

"Oh." She glanced away. "In Cambodia we like to have many children. Five is good. If you can support a lot of children and they healthy, you feel rich." . . .

They were quiet for a moment, then she spoke again.

"I have a lot of fun with my brother and sister, even if I act mad with them sometime. Samet have more freedom because he's a boy, and Mayoury, she the little one, so naturally she kind of get spoiled. But I'm just the middle daughter. So when my mother say she sending me to Réam, I say, 'Good, I be glad to get away.' But then I get homesick. You see how foolish? I have to go away before I see how I love my family."

"I guess that's the way it is with a lot of people. You know: Absence makes the heart grow fonder."

"Yes! That *exactly* how it is. The American understand this too, then!" She repeated it. "Absent make the heart grow fonder." She sighed. "That so true!"

"Look," he said, "if it's bothering you to talk about all this . . . "

She laughed shortly. "I say we shouldn't talk about, then I start again."

"You don't have to. Maybe I shouldn't have brought it up at all."

"No, that's okay. You know, I never talk about this before. Not to an American."

"Really?"

She nodded. "I don't mind telling, if you sure you want to hear."

"I do. Go on. How did you get out of Cambodia?"

She took a deep breath. "Well, my uncle is like a clerk for the U.S. government, and if the Communist get him that not gonna be good. . . ." She drew a finger across her throat. "So when we hear they coming we run down and get on the ship. Everybody say, 'Oh, we just stay away a couple day, let everything settle down.' But pretty soon some people come by in a little boat and say already they are killing. So we leave."

"And headed for America," Jonathan said thoughtfully.

"Oh, we not heading *for* anyplace. We just getting away from the killing. First we go to Thailand, then Malaysia, Indonesia . . . We don't know *where* we gonna end up. We just floating around like that for six, seven week. Finally the American let us come to a camp in the Philippine. We stay there awhile, then they bring us to California."

"I was asking my folks about this and they seemed to think everybody who left Vietnam and Cambodia in '75 was evacuated by our government. All nice and orderly, like it was planned ahead of time."

"No." She shook her head. "Nobody ever talk about leave Cambodia, not to me. My aunt and uncle never talk about 'Let's pack' or 'Better get ready.' Just pick up and go that day." She sighed. "I don't want to go. I want to go back to Phnom Penh because I'm so scared for my family, but my uncle say, 'Niece, no time to cry! Too late! Come on!'"

She paused. "Why you look at me that way?"

He shook his head. "God, I can't imagine having to leave my home like that, then try to go on with my life in some other country without knowing what had happened to my family."

"But as long as I don't hear they die, I still have hope." She made her voice light. "I know a Korean girl—her mother just find her sister again, almost thirty year since the war in Korea. Me, I'm only hoping four year so far!"

But Jonathan just stared at the ground. . . .

Of all the guests seated on their living room floor Sunday evening, Sundara was happiest to see her friend Moni.

"How lucky I feel," the round-faced older girl was saying now, "to sit down to your good food, Soka." Every time Moni came over she seemed a little plumper. "I don't care how fat I get," she had often told Sundara. After eating insects, rats, and scorpions to stay alive, a few extra pounds seemed like a smart idea.

Soka urged another plateful on her. "It helps, being able to glean for the garlic. When it's free, I don't have to be stingy with it. As for the rice, I just have to do the best I can with the pitiful stuff they sell here."

Grandmother sighed. "How I miss the rice we had at home, the way it always smelled so fresh. The kind we get here has all the goodness milled right out of it."

"I'm just thankful they have rice at all in America," Moni said. "I'm such a lobster brain, I had the notion they ate only bread!"

Sundara joined in the soft laughter. She liked the way Moni was never afraid to tell a joke on herself. After everything she'd been through, it was surprising she could laugh at all.

Back in Cambodia, Moni's young husband had been a soldier. Left alone while he fought the Communists, she'd taken refuge in Phnom Penh to await the birth of her baby—one among thousands, camping on the sidewalks. When the Khmer Rouge took the city, she, like many others, hoped for the best. Maybe the Communists would not be so bad. At least the fighting and killing would stop. And soon she could be with her husband again. For a brief hour or so as the truckloads of soldiers rumbled through the streets, people actually cheered.

But the mood of celebration did not last. Soon the soldiers were ordering everyone to leave the city. The Americans, they said, were coming in their B-52s to bomb Phnom Penh. Easy to believe. Hadn't the American search for lurking North Vietnamese already cratered much of the Cambodian countryside?

As the march from Phnom Penh began, Moni's time came, as the Khmer women say, to swim the Great River. On a sidewalk, with people trudging past, she gave birth. Soka and Sundara had wept to hear this, but Moni assured them she was not the only one. "And much worse things were happening. After my baby was born, a little boy begged me for help. He must have been one of those thrown out of the hospital because his foot . . . was gone. But I couldn't carry him. I was so weak myself and with my own new baby . . . Oiee, his little spirit comes to me still."

Naturally, Soka and Sundara assumed her baby had died; many Khmer babies failed to survive under much better conditions. Soka herself had lost two between Ravy and Pon. But Moni said no, she lived. "She was a strong little peasant, like me."

Not knowing which direction to walk, the city dwellers had been herded around the countryside by the dead-eyed, black-garbed soldiers.

But Moni plodded steadily north toward her parents' rice-farming village, baby tied in her *krama*. She ate whatever she could find, even tree bark, when she came across some that was free of the Americans' leaf-killing poison spray. At her parents' she recovered, but soon learned her husband would have been one of the first executed when the Khmer Rouge began their purge. And the new Kampuchea had no place for the widows of anti-Communist soldiers. She, too, was marked for death.

Leaving the baby with her parents, she fled on foot, her breasts aching with the milk her baby would never suck. Through the jungle she made her way, braving wild panthers and Khmer Rouge soldiers, picking around the mines and the scattered bones of those who'd chosen the wrong place to step. She'd even managed to sneak past the thieves at the Thai border.

Her story haunted Sundara. Such courage. Not only had Moni given birth to the child, but she kept it alive. How had Moni succeeded in this, where Sundara had failed? But Sundara's guilt about Soka's baby was something she could never discuss. Not even with Moni. . . .

Only a few weeks before she'd left the country forever, her father had given her the loveliest blue parasol painted with pink roses—not a good gift, as it turned out, to cheer a girl weary of remaining at home. How she'd pleaded with him to take her walking along the quay. In her mind she saw herself twirling it, drawing the attention of the boys on their bicycles. Of course, in her father's presence, she could hardly return their smiles, but how pleasant to see them watching her. And maybe she and Papa could stop at one of the Parisian-style cafés? Or take a pedicab ride to the Chinese shopping district?

"Innocent One, I cannot take you. It's too dangerous with the rockets. And believe me, the city is not as you remember it."

Hateful war. It ruined everything.

And now, in spite of everything she'd gone through in the months that followed, everything that showed her just how sheltered she'd been and how little she'd understood of the war, this one thought still haunted her: Never would she stroll the Boulevard Monivong beneath the lavender jacarandas[17] and blooming peacock trees, twirling a painted parasol. Not while her hair was still black, anyway, not

---

17. **jacarandas** tropical trees with showy flowers

while she was young and pretty. Shamefully foolish, this regret, but somehow she couldn't get rid of it. . . .

Now the talk turned, as it always must, to the problems of life in America. Why did they have to pay those social security taxes? Wasn't that what families were for? But smuggling money back to the ones at home, that was a problem too. They always wanted more. They thought America was heaven because everyone had a car. They didn't understand that everyone *had* to have a car. And speaking of cars, wasn't it terrible the looks they got for driving shiny new ones? They'd saved and paid cash, hadn't they? And bought American, too, not Japanese! There was no way to win. If they went on welfare, Americans called them spongers. If they worked hard and succeeded, people got jealous.

Among the guests were a man and wife newly arrived in America, and they listened, wide-eyed, as the others went on and on, saying the same things Sundara had heard so many times before. How strange all this must sound to them, she thought. Only a few weeks ago they'd been languishing in a squalid refugee camp, probably imagining America as the answer to every prayer.

Then again, Sundara thought, at least they'd been *wanting* to come here. Waiting, they'd had time to get used to the idea.

For her family, it had all happened with such bewildering speed. She had not known she was leaving her home, perhaps forever, that frantic April night when they boarded the ship. Not until two months later had it dawned on her this was not some temporary so-journ, a terrible but brief interlude until the trouble at home blew over. When it hit her, she was sitting in the tent of a hastily assem-bled orientation class at Camp Pendleton, California. *Heaven protect me*, she'd thought, her eyes glazing with sudden, stunned dismay. The teacher was explaining how to live in America—as if that's what they'd be doing for a long, long time. They were not going home, not soon. Maybe never. Good-bye Kampuchea, hello America. They'd made one conscious decision—to flee for their lives—and here they were. Just yesterday, it seemed, she'd been swinging on a breezy porch in a Cambodian fishing village, now she was sweltering in an armed camp guarded by rifle-toting American soldiers.

Still, Sundara thought now, looking at the newly arrived husband and wife, this family's long, idle months in the Thai camp were noth-ing to envy, and even with the support of fellow Khmers it would be harder for them in many ways, coming now. They could not have escaped with their savings in a few rubies, sapphires, or leaves of gold as Naro and some of the other first ones had, and no doubt they were already worn down with having suffered so many difficulties. . . .

Naro shook his head sadly. "I still cannot understand how it's come to this: People fleeing not only from the Vietnamese, but also from fellow Khmers. Our own people! The Vietnamese are not slaughtering each other."

Oh, stop, Sundara thought.

"It seems impossible," the new man offered quietly, "but many are saying the Vietnamese will be an improvement over the Khmer Rouge."

"What a choice! Like running from the tiger on the land and being eaten by the alligator in the water. The Vietnamese would be happy to see every Khmer starve so they could occupy our country permanently."

"Ah! If only Prince Sihanouk would come back."

They sighed with longing. Once, as a small child, Sundara had been part of the joyful throng that greeted Sihanouk on a wide, tree-lined boulevard in Phnom Penh. Her memories were not of the beloved ruler, however, but of the flowers everyone tossed at his slowly passing car, the necklace of fragrant jasmine she'd been given to wear in celebration. These older ones remembered Sihanouk himself, though. Somehow they thought if he could return from exile in China and rule Kampuchea once again, they might go home.

from
Old World Monkeys

Ann Elwood

In The Clay Marble, *a frightened refugee girl separated from her family wonders if the lone monkey confined in a military camp misses its family too. Unlike many baby animals who become independent quickly, a baby monkey may stay with its mother until it is three years old. Monkey families, like some human families, are being driven from their homes by forces beyond their control.*

MONKEYS SEEM TO BE a lot like us. They are curious. They show their feelings on their faces. And they have two arms and two legs, five fingers and five toes, and human-looking eyes and ears. This is not too surprising, because like us and our cousins the apes, monkey are primates[1] . . .

Scientists divide monkeys into two groups—*Old World monkeys* and *New World monkeys*. Old World monkeys live in Africa and Asia, mainly in rain forests and in woodland-grassland regions. They are different in several ways from New World monkeys, which live in Central and South America. For example, their nostrils are smaller and closer together, and some of them have callouses on their back ends like built-in seat cushions. Many New World monkeys have *prehensile* (pre-HEN-suhl) tails, tails that can grasp objects in much the same way that a hand can. But Old World monkeys do not have the prehensile tails.

On the surface, Old World monkeys *look* very different from each other. Some have faces that look like masks, others are bearded, and

---

1. **primates** the highest order of mammals

still others have crests on their heads. Some . . . have amazingly color-ful faces. Colobus monkeys have beautiful furry tails, but some mon-keys have tails that are so small you can barely see them. The biggest Old World monkeys are the drill and the mandrill, which can weigh up to 110 pounds (50 kilograms) each. The smallest is the talapoin, which weighs as little as $1^1/_2$ pounds (680 grams).

The 82 species of Old World monkeys come in a variety of shapes, sizes, and colors. In general, Old World monkeys can be divided into two subfamilies—the *cercopithecines* (sir-cuh-PITH-uh-ceens) and the *colobines* (COLL-uh-beans). The cercopithecines eat fruit and many other types of food, and they have big cheek pouches in which to carry it. The colobines are usually more slender, and they lack cheek pouches. Mainly leaf eaters, they have highly specialized stomachs to help them break down and di-gest their food.

The bodies of all monkeys evolved[2] for life in the trees. All monkeys have hands and feet that can grasp onto branches. And their eyes, like ours, are made for seeing things in three dimensions. This is especially important for tree dwellers, which need to judge distances from branch to branch and from branch to ground.

The ways in which monkeys' bodies differ from species to species has a lot to do with where they live and what they eat. For example, tree-dwelling

Monkey with long tail on tree branch: De Brazza's Monkey *Cercopithecines neglectus (Cercopithecine)*

monkeys have limber[3] bodies that are perfect for leaping between

---

2. **evolved** developed to a more highly organized condition
3. **limber** bending easily

branches. And ground-dwelling monkeys have shorter, more robust[4] bodies built for surviving on the ground.

Monkey babies get lots of love and attention. When a baby is born, members of the troop are quick to come and see it. Monkey

Mother and baby: *Hanuman Langur Presbytis entellus (Colobine)*

mothers usually have only one baby at a time. The baby's eyes are open at birth, and it has fur. Though quite helpless in most other ways, it is born with the ability to cling to its mother with its hands and feet. Being able to cling is very useful for a baby whose mother uses her hands and feet to get around in the trees.

Monkey children have long childhoods—sometimes lasting up to 3 years. When they are very young, the babies stay close to their mothers. Then, as they grow older, they begin to play with other young monkeys. They chase each other, pull each other's tails, and play follow-the-leader. By playing together, young monkeys learn how to live in a group. And they develop physical skills that are important for life on the ground and in the trees.

Monkeys behave in ways that help them to survive. Because they lack horns, scales, poisons, fighting ability, and other forms of self-defense, they rely mostly on their wits to stay out of danger. As a group, monkeys learn quickly and adapt easily to new situations. And

---

4. **robust** hardy

for this reason, they are very successful animals.

Monkeys are also very social animals. They live together in groups called *troops*. But some monkeys live in larger troops than others. Gelada (juh-LAH-duh) monkeys, for instance, . . . sometimes band together in huge troops of several hundred animals. By sticking close together, monkeys have a better chance of detecting predators such as snakes, lions, hyenas, cheetahs, leopards, people, and other primates.

Some cultures worship monkeys, and others treat them badly. But no matter what the human attitude is, many monkeys are in danger because their habitat[5] is shrinking.

Cultures that worship monkeys protect them from harm. But in other cultures, monkeys are hunted for their fur and for meat. They are killed for the stones in their stomachs, which people use as medicine. And they are destroyed by farmers who catch them raiding their crops.

Still, the biggest danger to monkeys is loss of habitat. And many species, especially those that live in rain forests, are endangered because of this. Special land has been set aside for monkeys in many parts of Asia and Africa. But this is only the first step toward saving them.

---

5. **habitat** area where an animal or plant naturally lives or grows

Hannelore Schäl
and Ulla Abdalla

from
Toys Made of Clay

Clay is available almost everywhere there is soil and water. It is easily worked into shapes by hand. Clay is one of the natural substances that Jantu, the youthful artist in The Clay Marble, *uses to create artwork that entertains the other refugee children. Some of the techniques she uses in manipulating her clay creations are described in this selection.*

Clay Is a Small Piece of Earth

There are different kinds of clay.

Clay is made from finely ground rocks. Over many millions of years, these rocks have been brought from the mountains into the valleys by wind and water. Today we find various clay deposits,[1] depending on the color of the original rocks. Clay can be red, yellow, gray, black, or white.

Where to buy clay

Clay can be bought in pottery stores or in handicraft stores.

- The clay you buy is all ready to use. You can start right in making things with it.

- You may find clay in your own yard; clay is almost everywhere. When you find clay, you can try to make some little toys from it and just let the clay dry without having it fired in a kiln.[2]

---

1. **deposits** natural layers of a mineral
2. **kiln** oven used in making bricks or pottery

Wedging

Sometimes the clay has air pockets. Then the clay must be pounded or thrown (wedged) to get these out. Throw the piece of clay firmly against a board or on a tabletop several times.

How to cut off a piece of clay

Put a string around the middle of your piece of clay. Cross the ends of the string and pull tightly to cut the clay in half. Put the clay you are not using into a plastic bag and close the bag tightly so that the clay won't dry out.

How to shape clay

Only soft clay can be shaped. Clay shrinks a bit and gets hard when it dries . . .

How to moisten dried-out clay

Add some water to dry or leftover pieces and knead[3] thoroughly.

- *Too-dry Clay:* Make holes in the clay. Fill with water, let stand, then knead.
- *Hardened Clay:* Put into water to soften. Then knead.
- *Too-wet Clay:* Let dry in air for a while, then knead.

Drying clay toys

Clay should dry slowly. Cover your clay toys with plastic sheets and let them dry in a cool place. Small clay pieces need one week to dry. Big pieces need two weeks.

Firing

The dried clay pieces can be fired in a kiln. Kilns are available in pottery stores. (CAUTION: Do not try to use a kiln yourself. Have an adult do the firing for you.)

---

3. **knead** press and squeeze with the hands

The Best Way to Do It

You will need: A wooden board or a plastic bag to work on, some wooden sticks, a rolling pin or a bottle, some newspaper.

To attach clay pieces to each other

If pieces of clay are not firmly attached to each other, they fall apart. Small pieces fall off easily if they are not attached properly. So press the pieces together as firmly as possible and smear a thin clay "slip" between the pieces smoothly, so that no crack can be seen.

A slip

Make a slip by adding water to the clay and stirring until you have a paste.

Smooth it out

Smooth out the clay between the parts. Or make small coils[4] of clay, put them around the joints, and press them smooth.

Joints between two parts must always be smoothed over.

Pieces of clay that are thicker than 1 inch crack in the kiln. Hollow out thicker pieces or make holes underneath the piece with a small stick or a knitting needle.

To hollow out clay

Use your fingers or a spoon to dig out clumps of clay. Make sure the walls of your dish are of equal thickness (1/2 to 1 inch) when you finish hollowing out.

If you take too much clay from the sides when you are hollowing out, just smear fresh clay on the area as you need it.

To roll out clay

Press the lump of clay flat, then roll it with a rolling pin or a bottle, keeping the thickness as even as possible.

---

4. **coils** rings

To make a hollow clay ball

Flatten a lump of clay with your fist. Make two of these and wrap them around a crumpled ball of newspaper. Blend the clay well between pieces. Continue to put flat pieces of clay over the paper ball until it is completely covered.

When to paint clay

After your clay figures have completely dried and/or have been fired, they are ready to be painted.

Painting tip: Use a lacquer[5] (or shellac) over your colors, or use lacquer paint. The finish will be glossy and waterproof.

---

5. **lacquer** fast-drying varnish

The Shaping of *The Clay Marble*

Minfong Ho

Before Minfong Ho could write about the Cambo-dian refugees, she had to face the memories of her own experiences with them. This memoir tells how a pine tree's breaking in a snow storm led to The Clay Marble.

THERE IS A MASSIVE, old white pine that grows in a corner of our backyard here in upstate New York. Its boughs shade a sandbox where our two toddlers played, its lower branches held a precarious[1] tree house they built, and its needles provided a soft bed where I could read. Its effortless symmetry[2] hinted of a stability and permanence that has always calmed me.

One winter morning, after a heavy snowstorm, the lowest branch of this old pine suddenly broke off, under the burden of the new snow. From the kitchen window, I heard a loud splintering sound, then the crash as it hit the ground, tearing apart the tree house, crushing the little sandbox. I rushed outside to look at the tree. There, in the tree trunk where the branch had ripped off, was a dark, deep rot, so soft that I could have plunged my hand in and scooped out moist pulp. It looked as if the tree was rotten to its core. I stared at it and thought: that's me.

Why?

After all, hadn't things been going well for me: graduate school, marriage, children, and now our own house? So why did it feel so wrong?

If I had to answer that in one word, I would say now, "Cambodia." But I did not realize it then. That winter, Cambodia was as hidden and buried in me as the rot in the old pine tree.

---

1. **precarious** insecure; dangerously unsteady
2. **symmetry** balance of form or proportion

I am not Cambodian, had not even ever set foot in Cambodia all the first fifteen years that I grew up in neighboring Thailand. All I had done was to do some relief work on the Thai-Cambodian border in 1980, when the first influx[3] of refugees from the harsh Pol Pot[4] regime started to straggle into Thailand.

The work itself was straightforward enough. I was supposed to help set up supplementary[5] feeding centers for the severely malnourished children in the ring of refugee camps along the Thai border. Basically, this consisted of buying truckloads of fresh vegetables and rice and charcoal, getting the stuff to the thatched kitchens at far-flung sites, and overseeing the distribution of the cooked food to the long lines of children waiting under the hot sun. It was time-consuming work, and tiring, but not particularly difficult. Plenty of other people—the surgeons and nurses, the UNICEF[6] field staff, even the military patrol—had much more grueling jobs, which they seemed to perform efficiently, unflinchingly.

And yet I hadn't been able to do my work properly. I remember being erratic,[7] moody, angry, morose,[8] an emotional minefield. Most nights I would cry myself to sleep . . . .

Eventually I quit and returned to graduate school at Cornell, and resumed "normal" life.

Until the big old pine tree broke.

My husband called up his good friend Robin, a tree surgeon. I sought out another friend, Rachel, a motherly Jewish therapist who had fled her childhood home in Europe just before the Second World War.

Robin the tree surgeon took a look at the tree and said: let it be, it's strong and tough, it'll heal itself.

Rachel the therapist took a look at me and said, predictably enough, "Talk."

It was very difficult to talk about Cambodia, about the Cambodian refugees. Without my having acknowledged it, I had

---

3. **influx** continuous coming in
4. **Pol Pot** Communist leader of Cambodia whose government from 1975–1979 caused an estimated 2 million deaths from mass evacuations, forced labor, starvation, disease, torture, or execution
5. **supplementary** additional
6. **UNICEF** United Nations International Children's Emergency Fund; now known as United Nations Children's Fund
7. **erratic** irregular in mood or movement
8. **morose** gloomy

been sucked into the conspiracy[9] of silence that is so often generated by absolute misery. The Cambodian refugees themselves had not spoken much of their own suffering. How could I? One does not talk about such unspeakable things.

I remembered, yes, but I did not want to, could not, talk—about the dead and the dying, the starving and the shooting, the pain and the suffering, and most terrible of all, the total senselessness of it. Why had it happened? Why was it still happening? And why was it inflicted onto even the children? How could such things be talked about?

The Cambodians that I saw were for the most part themselves silent. Especially in the malnutrition "wards," no more than makeshift thatched huts, where I spent a lot of my time, the children were too weak to cry, their mothers too stoic[10] or perhaps too tired to talk. It was a terrible thing, this silence, like some thick web that had descended and choked everyone underneath.

Only very rarely was the silence ever broken. And when that happened, it too would be terrible. I remember once hearing some screaming outside the ward I was working in. Two Cambodian women were standing in the fierce noonday sun, fighting and screaming at each other. One of them had evidently been a Khmer Rouge cadre[11] in the Pol Pot regime, while the other was someone who must have suffered horribly under that same regime. The latter was crying: how could you have killed so many of us, how could you have been so cruel? The Khmer Rouge ex-cadre was screaming back, in equal anguish:[12] how could you have *let* us do this to you?

Nothing made any sense, not the silence, not the screams.

"But you don't have to be silent," Rachel said, "and you don't have to scream. Try talking." And so I started talking.

I told her how seeing the Cambodian refugees on the Border had shaken me to the core of my being. Growing up in Bangkok I had often seen beggars on the streets, or malnourished babies of nomadic[13] hill tribes in northern Thailand, but never, never in all my life had I seen such absolute misery, on such a massive[14] scale.

---

9. **conspiracy** acting together; agreement
10. **stoic** calm and unflinching under suffering
11. **cadre** member of a political leadership unit, especially Communist
12. **anguish** great suffering; agony
13. **nomadic** wandering
14. **massive** large

In one border camp there had been tall watchtowers of split bamboo erected. If you climbed to the top of this watchtower, you would see thousands, hundreds of thousands of people, like a churning brown ocean, stretched out in every direction as far as the eye could see. All of them uprooted, helpless, and silent. It was overwhelming.

Yet seeing the refugees somehow confirmed one of my most deep-rooted fears: that one's regular, mundane[15] life could be so suddenly and drastically disrupted. Growing up in a Chinese immigrant family as I did, I was used to hearing stories of how, for example, my mother had left her childhood home in Shanghai blithely[16] one summer and was never able to return, because the Japanese had taken it over. When she was finally able to go back, almost forty years later, the house had been razed[17] to the ground. She had not even been able to locate her mother's gravesite. Most of our friends and family of her generation have similar stories to tell. Or I would be told how after I was born in Burma, my parents left Rangoon "temporarily" with me so that my mother could give birth to my brother in the relative comfort of Hong Kong and how we had never gone back to Burma because of the political turmoil there. As a result, neither my mother nor I have many photos of ourselves as young children, because our childhood photographs, together with other family possessions, had all been irrevocably[18] left behind.

The lives of these Cambodian refugees had been disrupted in much the same way. Like us, they had been living quietly one day, with the rumblings of war only a distant reality, and the next day everything had changed. They had to move, and they had to leave behind not only a lifetime of possessions, but everything they were familiar with—language, culture, religion, country. In a very literal way, none of us could ever go home again.

I think, in retrospect,[19] I had always felt a dread of such sudden disruption in my life. It meant that I could have very little control over my own destiny, because the big things—when I might be uprooted and where I might be able to go afterwards—were completely beyond my control. This is not humility; it is a sense of enforced helplessness.

---

15. **mundane** everyday; ordinary
16. **blithely** cheerfully; in a carefree manner
17. **razed** torn down completely
18. **irrevocably** unalterably; not able to be changed
19. **in retrospect** in reviewing the past

Then, too, I felt that the fate of these refugees touched close to home because they were very much like people I grew up with in neighboring Thailand. I speak Thai, and can therefore understand many Cambodian words that have the same Sanskrit-based roots. And their clothing, the dances, the Buddhist religion, all seemed familiar to me because they were so closely linked with Thailand's own traditions. And, basically, I identified with them simply because I looked like them.

There was one camp that I visited early on during my time on the Border that was secluded[20] and heavily guarded, because many of the refugees inside it were ethnic Chinese[21] from Cambodia. Since my own mother-tongue is Chinese, I had felt an instant rapport[22] with these refugees, listening to their stories of escape and loss. The afternoon passed quickly, and before I knew it the Thai security guards were ushering out the handful of foreign relief workers in preparation to locking up the camp. My colleagues all left, but the security guards wouldn't let me out because they thought, quite understandably, that I was one of the refugees. No amount of argument on my part, whether it was in Thai, in Chinese, or in English, would persuade the guards that I actually belonged outside. It finally took one of my fellow relief workers, a white man—and therefore visibly foreign—to vouch for me and to insist that they let me go. As I walked out and the gates slammed behind me, I remember feeling a great disquiet,[23] that perhaps I really belonged in there with Them instead of outside with the foreign Us.

That same sense of dislocation[24] stayed with me after I left the Border altogether: what was I doing in upstate New York, pretending that the Thai-Cambodian border and the refugees never existed? Why wasn't I back there with them? Why did my life now seem a farce,[25] unreal and shadowy, when the nightmare of the Border by contrast seemed so real?

I talked and talked, as Rachel listened. Once in a while she would murmur something. "Post-Traumatic Stress Syndrome," she said once.

---

20. **secluded** shut off; isolated
21. **ethnic Chinese** people with a Chinese background or heritage
22. **rapport** close, sympathetic relationship
23. **disquiet** uneasy feeling
24. **dislocation** being out of place
25. **farce** something absurd; ridiculous; an obvious pretense

"Read Eli Wiesel[26]," she suggested.

Post-what?

Eli who?

Eli Wiesel. There was a whole shelf of his books at the public library. I took out the first one of the lot ("Accident, The"). All I knew about him was what it said on the dust jacket of the book, that the author had survived the Holocaust at Auschwitz as a young man. The story opened with someone who narrowly escaped death after being hit by a car but who felt afterwards that he had really no right to be alive. I don't remember details, just that I could not stop reading, could not stop crying. By the end of the book it was dusk, the box of tissues was all used up, and I was exhausted.

But also more at peace. There was a feeling of overwhelming relief, that someone else had actually felt this way, had felt so devastated by death that life could seem only an obscene mockery of it. Yet there was a shaft of hope—the very fact that this writer, this survivor, had voiced his deep despair with such control hinted at some indomitable[27] wellspring[28] of strength and yes, even beauty.

I understood then that between the silence and the scream, there could be a song.

More than anything, I wanted to find the song in the refugee camps of the Border. And to do that, I had to face the refugees again.

I pulled out cardboard boxes of journals I had haphazardly written in while I was working on the Border, looked at photographs I had taken of the people there. I opened myself to the people in my notebooks, in my photographs, and in my memory. I let them talk, and I tried to hear what they might be saying to me.

It was the children who spoke to me most directly. They had made me so uneasy for so long, keeping their silent vigil in my mind. I didn't know, still don't know, what it was that made them stay there, waiting, watching. Were they sad? Angry? Sullen? Envious? What did they want of me? Why did they want to talk to me? Did they want me to understand, to remember, to give them voice, movement, life? What was it in them, in me, that wouldn't let them just gently disappear? Did they hate me? Did I hate them? Did I love them? What if they needed me? Why did I need them? Why couldn't they talk to me?

---

26. **Elie Wiesel** Romanian-born American novelist and winner of the 1986 Nobel Prize for Peace
27. **indomitable** not easily defeated; unconquerable
28. **wellspring** source of abundant and continual supply

What could they have said? I hate you I need you I hurt I can't bear it I am bearing it go away stay come back touch me hold me leave me alone? And how could I have said any of that either? Even while I was with them at the Border, I had been unable to really talk to them. Instead I had cooked and trucked food around and fed them, maintaining that silence, that unbridgeable distance. And every day that I kept it up I had known it was a sham.[29] I was ashamed, ashamed of being so useless, so weak, so well-fed myself. How could I live with so much, when they had nothing?

And yet, of course, there was really no Them, no Me. I was Them, each child, each barefoot, snotnosed child. I had been so much like them, when I was little. I knew them, was familiar with them, and most devastating of all, I liked them, liked their gumption,[30] their spirit, their sudden giggles. If I had been ten or fifteen years younger, I would have wanted nothing more than to be friends with them. Instead, separated by a few years and an arbitrary[31] twist of history, we had diverged into such different paths: they to endure war and famine, I to watch them endure. But they *had* endured, these sweet tough children, tougher by far than I could ever be. They had endured; I had cracked under the strain of just watching them endure.

It was this endurance, the memory of their resilience,[32] that spoke to me now. I examined the faces of the children in my photographs, and surprisingly many of them were smiling, even laughing. I had never been able to bring myself to point my camera into the faces of the sick and miserable, since that would have violated what little they had left of themselves. But there amidst the images of ugliness and suffering that had haunted me, I found that there *had* been flashes of happiness.

Tenuous[33] at first as the first blades of new grass after a hard drought, these memories of hope began to surface. I remembered the ingenious[34] toys the children at the refugee camps had made: fish woven from strips of plastic IV tubes, trucks from tin cans, and everywhere the little dolls and animals shaped from clay.

29. **sham** pretense
30. **gumption** courage and initiative
31. **arbitrary** not fixed by rules; based on a whim
32. **resilience** ability to bounce back, to recover quickly
33. **tenuous** slender; flimsy
34. **ingenious** clever

And out of the dreaded silence I remembered some sounds of laughter. Once, in a malnutrition ward, I was sitting next to a stick-thin baby held in the lap of his older sister, herself no more than eight or ten years old. On her wrist were several rubber bands, and I had gently pulled one and snapped it against her arm. Playfully, she had reached over to the rubber band on my own wrist (which I used to tie back my hair) and snapped it against me. I laughed; she giggled. It was a lovely light sound, her giggle. Soon there was a small crowd of little girls gathered around me, taking turns to snap my rubber band and holding up their wrists for me to snap theirs. For a moment, the sound of their light laughter filled the ward. How had I forgotten that?

And, too, I remembered a gift another little girl had given me one day. For no reason that I could see, a ragged little girl had come over and slipped something into my hand. It was a clay marble, so smooth that she must have spent hours rolling it between her palms. Briefly, we linked fingers, our skin so much the same shade of brown that we could easily have been sisters.

And thinking of that marble again, I realized that if she could shape such a lovely round marble out of the chaos of her own life, then I too would try and shape something out of my own confusion.

And so I followed her example and started to shape my own clay marble.

Writing the story *The Clay Marble* was not an easy process, but it was a slow, healing one. I started moulding it around the girl who gave me her clay marble, naming her Dara, and eventually she took over the whole story. At the time I was writing, I had not known the word *empowerment*, but looking back on it, I think that was what happened to Dara, and through her to myself.

One of the deepest satisfactions came after the story was almost finished. My husband had accepted a job in Laos, and so we moved back to Southeast Asia, our two young children in tow. Living for a year in Laos—Cambodia's Communist neighbor—I could sense for myself the basic peace and stability of the countryside.

I visited Cambodia too and spent time not only in its capital city of Phnom Penh, but also its surrounding countryside.

It had been over a decade since the turmoil of the Communist takeover there, after the vast outflow of refugees, and in the aftermath of the dislocation there was still widespread poverty. Yet both in Laos and in Cambodia life had resumed its age-old pattern. Men ploughed their paddy fields, young monks swept temple compounds, looms clicked as women wove checkered sarongs[35] underneath stilted houses. And the children, like the children everywhere, were spinning tops, flying kites, making marbles out of clay.

It was in Laos that I finished up the revisions for *The Clay Marble* and wrote the final two pages. When I turned those in to my editor at faraway Farrar, Straus and Giroux, I said in my letter to her:

> It has been a gift, to be able to finish up the story here, with the swallows diving in arcs above the rice fields right outside my window, the mango trees a stone's throw from my desk. Everything is a seamless whole, the fields, the story, the past, the present, Dara, myself.
>
> I could not have envisioned before, how life goes on, after the misery and suffering I saw on the Border. The last glimpse I had, of children like Dara, was of their oxcarts, heading past the land mined forests, to a war torn country. And now, I have met them on the other end. The countryside here, behind the "rattan curtain" in Indochina, is very poor, but— and this makes all the difference in the world for me—I find the children playing here, as I did on the Border.
>
> I did not make it all up, it was not some solipsistic[36] nightmare I had, shut up in a cold house in upstate New York. It all happened, it exists, it is all here. I have come home again, and I have brought Dara and her family home with me. And now finally I can leave her safely here.

That was a couple of years ago, and now here I am back at that same "cold house in upstate New York." Instead of rice fields, my desk now overlooks that big old pine tree in the backyard.

We have taken the advice of the tree surgeon and let the old white pine alone, rather than dredge[37] out the rot or seal over the hole with cement. And just as Robin said, it was a tough old thing; its trunk and its own root system keep growing, and it is healing itself.

All through this morning the snow has been falling heavily, and the world outside my window is a whirl of white. The massive boughs

---

35. **sarongs** garments consisting of long strips of cloth, often brightly colored and printed, worn like a skirt
36. **solipsistic** self-absorbed
37. **dredge** dig or scoop

of the pine tree are completely covered now, and the lowest branch is so heavily weighed down with snow that the tips of it are touching the ground, forming a sort of lacy igloo under the tree. I will go out now and shake some of the snow off that branch.

Because, as Rachel maintains, even the strongest and toughest things can do with a bit of help, now and then.

DATE DUE
